"Trust me when I say there are way worse things than pretending to date a pretty woman."

Had Cole just called her pretty? Even if he wasn't thinking romantic thoughts toward her, that simple comment filled her with a joy that wasn't wise but which there was no stopping.

"Well, I better get home," she said as she reached for the door handle.

"Wait," he said. He hopped out of the truck and hurried over to her side to open the door.

"This isn't necessary," she said when she allowed him to hold her hand as she slipped out of the truck. "No one is around."

He glanced beyond her for a moment then started to lower his head toward her.

Oh, my God! He's going to kiss me. Her heart thumped hard.

But in the next moment, he whispered in her ear, "Your parents just walked out of La Cantina."

"Oh," she managed, perhaps a bit too disappointed.

Who was she kidding? She *was* disappointed. What had she gotten herself into?

Dear Reader,

Welcome back to Blue Falls, Texas, and another tale of happily-ever-after. The more I build and populate Blue Falls with characters, the more I grow to love it. These cowboys and ranchers and the women who love them while living amazing lives of their own are so real to me, and I hope it's the same for you, the reader.

While *The Cowboy Takes a Wife* finally brings to fruition Blue Falls's new Arts and Crafts Trail, which you've been reading about in the past few books, there are so many more stories of love in this Hill Country town to tell. As I write this letter, I'm already brainstorming new Blue Falls stories. I hope you are eagerly awaiting reading them as much as I am writing them.

I love to hear from readers. Let me know what you like about Blue Falls, maybe even whose story you'd like to see next. You can email me through my website at trishmilburn.com with your comments. And as always, thanks to the moon and back for your support.

Trish Milburn

THE COWBOY
TAKES A WIFE

—

TRISH MILBURN

Recycling programs
for this product may
not exist in your area.

ISBN-13: 978-0-373-75732-9

The Cowboy Takes a Wife

Copyright © 2016 by Trish Milburn

Printed in U.S.A.

Trish Milburn writes contemporary romance for the Harlequin Western Romance line. She's a two-time Golden Heart® Award winner, a fan of walks in the woods and road trips, and a big geek girl, including being a dedicated Whovian and Browncoat. And from her earliest memories, she's been a fan of Westerns, be they historical or contemporary. There's nothing quite like a cowboy hero.

Books by Trish Milburn

Harlequin American Romance

Elly: Cowgirl Bride
The Texan's Cowgirl Bride

Blue Falls, Texas

Her Perfect Cowboy
Having the Cowboy's Baby
Marrying the Cowboy
The Doctor's Cowboy
Her Cowboy Groom
The Heart of a Cowboy
Home on the Ranch
A Rancher to Love

The Teagues of Texas

The Cowboy's Secret Son
Cowboy to the Rescue
The Cowboy Sheriff

Visit the Author Profile page at Harlequin.com for more titles.

Chapter One

Devon Newberry placed the skein of bright orange yarn and a dozen vanilla-scented candles in the paper bag and handed it across the counter to Merline Teague.

"Thanks so much," Devon said as she smiled at the older woman, the mom of local sheriff Simon Teague and his two brothers.

"No, thank you, dear. Your candles keep the gallery smelling wonderful."

"I'm glad. I need to get by there soon. I haven't been in a while."

"Oh, you should come by next week. We're having an opening for a new exhibit of art created by students at the high school. I'm just in awe of the talent they have."

"That sounds wonderful. I'll try to find some time to see it."

"Speaking of, I better run. I still have a lot of work to do to prepare. Thanks again," Merline said as she lifted her bag and headed toward the door of Devon's shop, A Good Yarn.

Devon sank onto the stool behind the cash register, grateful to get off her feet for a moment. The shop had been busy all afternoon, which was wonderful but also tiring. And she still had to prep the daily deposit and attend a meeting at the Blue Falls Tourist Bureau about the new Arts and Crafts Trail. But she wasn't going to complain about having a rush of customers, not when the fear of being an abject failure was as fresh now as it'd been when she'd opened her shop on Blue Falls' Main Street. Not when her mother's assertion that she was making a stupid mistake still echoed in her mind if she let it.

No, she was beyond thankful that the turning of the seasons to autumn put people in the mood to buy knitting supplies, hand-dipped candles and the various other homey touches Devon offered, even though the temperatures were still in the upper eighties during the day.

She let her gaze drift over the variety of displays she'd taken great care to create in order to best showcase both the products she made herself and those she chose from other sources. A well of pride rose within her. She was closing in on the two-year anniversary for A Good Yarn and felt like celebrating. She needed to plan a special event to bring loads of people into the shop that day.

She glanced at the clock on the wall, surprised by how late it was. Planning for her own event would have to wait until after the meeting about the one already in the works. As she stood, she thought maybe it could even wait until tomorrow. After the Arts and Crafts Trail meeting, she just might have a date with a luxurious bath and a good book.

She was in the midst of completing the day's tally and mentally picking out what book she wanted to read during her bath when her cell phone rang. When she saw the display, her good mood evaporated. And then she felt guilty about her immediate reaction. She shouldn't feel dread when faced with having to talk to her mother.

But then, most people probably didn't anticipate disapproval every time they talked to their moms, either.

Not wanting to be late for the meeting, she ignored the call and let it go to voice mail. With the bank deposit in hand, she blew out the pumpkin-spice candle and headed out the door, locking it behind her.

After a quick zip to the bank to make the deposit, she walked down the street to the Tourist Bureau office. The parking lot was full of vehicles, and several people were still making their way inside. Looked like a nice turnout, which was good since the self-guided trail that was to lead tourists from one artist's or craftsperson's gallery or shop to the next throughout the county was set to launch in mid-October, just in time for holiday shoppers. From the moment Gina Tolbert, executive director of the Tourist Bureau, had floated the idea to Devon, she'd known she wanted A Good Yarn to be a part of the trail. She was all for anything that brought attention to local artists and people who created products through sustainable means.

She said hello to Ella Garcia and her fiancé, Austin Bryant, as she made her way into the crowded entryway. As she scooted past a knot of people who'd paused to chat, she bumped into someone.

"Oh, I'm so sorry," she said as she turned to see whom she'd nearly bowled over. And had to look up, right into the bright blue eyes of Cole Davis.

She swallowed as her brain chose that moment to forget its job.

"Are you okay?"

Huh? Did he say something? *Oh good grief, you're acting like an idiot, like an awkward teenager with a crush on the high school quarterback.* Yes, she'd been that awkward teen, but Cole hadn't been the quarterback. No, he'd been the star of the school's rodeo team, and then he'd ridden his way onto the pro circuit.

"Uh, yeah," she said, her brain finally remembering she was supposed to say something. "Fine." She glanced around the room, pretending that she wasn't flustered. "Crowded in here."

"Devon, honey, good to see you." Barbara Davis stepped up beside her son, all smiles as usual. She looked like the perfect grandmother, only without the grandchildren.

"You, too."

Barbara motioned toward a row of chairs about halfway back the meeting room. "I found us some seats."

Devon saw that there were three empty chairs midway down the row and realized Barbara meant for Devon to join them. Since she couldn't come up with a polite way to refuse, she headed for the designated spot, intending to take the farthest chair so she'd have Barbara between her and Cole. Her plan was foiled a moment after Devon stepped past the first people in the row to reach her seat.

"You go next, Cole," Barbara said. "If you sit in the other chair, poor Ella won't be able to see anything but your back."

Devon looked at the row behind her and noticed that Ella and Austin had indeed found seats there. Too late to make a change now without looking like a flake. Oh well, she'd just concentrate on what Gina had to say and start brainstorming ideas for her anniversary celebration.

But when Cole sank onto the chair next to her a few seconds later, she realized that if she left this meeting knowing one word Gina or anyone else said, it would be a miracle worthy of the name.

Never had she found concentrating so difficult. She focused all her attention on Gina and the report of how many participants were signed up to take part in the trail—currently fifteen—but then Cole shifted beside her. He rubbed his large, tanned, powerful-looking hand down his jean-clad thigh, and she could swear she gulped loud enough to be heard in Oklahoma.

That thigh had gripped the side of countless mean bulls during his years on the pro rodeo circuit. She remembered happening upon a competition on TV once. She'd nearly brought blood to her lip from biting it as he rode. When he'd been tossed through the air as if he weighed no more than a gnat and slammed into the dirt of the arena, she'd actually cried out, startling her cat so much that Honeysuckle had fled into the next room.

Devon dragged her attention back to what Gina was saying, something about how the trail was going to be laid out. Doing her best to ignore the man beside her, Devon made a point of taking notes on a small notepad. But she would swear she could feel Cole's body heat. Or was that her own body temperature going whacko? It was as if he was giving off a megadose of pheromones. And for a guy who worked on a ranch, around cows and horses, he sure did smell good. Like he'd just stepped out from a shower and dried off with a fresh towel straight from the dryer.

She mentally rolled her eyes. Honestly, it wasn't as if she never saw the man. Granted, that was usually from a safe distance.

She dragged her thoughts back to the presentation again, raising her hand when Gina asked who all was willing to do a prize giveaway on the inaugural trail weekend. Out of the corner of her eye, Devon noticed Barbara raise her hand, as well. Whoever won one of

Barbara's handmade quilts would be one lucky duck. The woman was very skilled with needle and thread and with coming up with original designs.

Devon was confused, however, when Barbara tapped her son's hand, indicating he should raise his, as well. Did that mean Barbara was going to do two giveaways? That was beyond supportive of the town's new venture. When Cole started to say something, Barbara shushed him as if he were still a little boy. He obediently raised his hand.

Not wanting to show how humorous she found the entire mother-son exchange, Devon pressed her lips together to keep from laughing. How cute was a guy who still minded his mama.

Stop thinking about how cute he is. Think of something else, anything else!

Like how his high school girlfriend and eventual wife, Amy Frost, had been a complete witch to Devon back when the three of them had attended Blue Falls High. Those interactions were proof that it didn't matter how much money you had. If someone didn't think you dressed the right way, liked the right things, befriended the right classmates, they could make your life miserable.

Of course, thinking about Amy led to a memory of Cole during that same period, a memory that had taken on enormous importance to her teenage self. Maybe it still held more than it should.

"I swear, Devon, you were born into the wrong family," Amy had said as she sat nearly glued to Cole's side at their lunch table. She made a dismissive gesture toward Devon's loose cotton boho pants and oversize sweater. "You have the money to buy great clothes and you come to school looking like you picked through the donation bin at church."

Devon swallowed hard, trying not to cry. Could she stop Amy's barbs if she'd just wear the things her mother constantly brought home to her from Austin or San Antonio? No, she just couldn't do it, and not only because the outfits were totally not her style. Her mother was also oblivious to the fact that they weren't even the right size. The pants and dresses and stylish tops were made for a person three sizes smaller than Devon. It made her want to scream every time a new shopping bag showed up on her bed. What was ironic was a lot of those items ended up at the same church clothes' closet Amy accused her of frequenting as a recipient.

"Cut it out, Amy."

Devon's heart skipped a bit. Had she heard Cole correctly? Had he just defended her? Not only was he so gorgeous it made Devon want to weep, but he was gallant, as well.

More evidence that Devon wasn't like other kids her age. How many of them even had the word *gallant* enter their brains if it wasn't part of their homework?

"Any questions?"

Gina's voice and the rustling of people around her brought Devon back to the present. Heat rushed to her face because she'd allowed herself to get sucked back to those awkward, not-very-happy days of high school, complete with the accompanying feelings. She was annoyed that she had to remind herself that she wasn't the person she'd been back then.

She glanced briefly to her right, to where Cole was pushing himself to his feet. How much of the person that Cole had been in high school still resided in him? Or had a life on the road away from Blue Falls, and eventually away from Amy, made him into a man who didn't really resemble his younger self?

Devon shook her head and grabbed her purse. She didn't have any business wondering such things. She'd worked hard to craft a life for herself that she enjoyed, and she didn't need a man to make her complete. Though she couldn't seem to get that through her mother's head.

Along with just about everything else about herself. Her business, her clothes, her hairstyle, where she lived—you name it, her mom had something to say about it. Typically critical.

Once Devon was standing, she made eye contact with Barbara. "I take it you're going to take part in the trail with your quilts."

"Yes. I have a list of design ideas as long as my arm. But we mainly came for Cole."

Devon continued to stare at Barbara, confused.

Barbara chuckled. "That look on your face says I was right to bring this one along tonight." She patted Cole's upper arm. "We need to get the word out about his sculptures."

Sculptures? Devon was sure her confusion had left furrows on her forehead so deep you could plant crops in them.

"Turns out he has a real talent for making these beautiful metal sculptures," Barbara said.

"Mom," Cole said, sounding a little embarrassed.

Devon barely suppressed another grin.

"I don't know that *beautiful* is the right word," Cole said as he shifted his gaze to Devon. "I just weld together old scrap pieces that nobody wants."

"Pfftt," Barbara said with a dismissive wave. "Don't

listen to him. I stick by my assertion that his work is beautiful. You should come out to see it sometime."

Devon caught her mouth before it fell open. The last thing she needed to do was spend more time with Cole. At least not until she managed to purge her brain of those long-ago memories of him and got used to seeing him around town again. She knew he'd been back living on his family's ranch with his mom for a few months, but she'd probably seen only him twice.

You know it was twice—once at the Primrose Café and once when he'd been talking with Liam Parrish outside the hardware store.

She'd heard he'd retired from the rodeo circuit, but that was about it. And she hadn't been about to start asking questions about him. That would draw too much unwanted attention and questions directed back at her.

"Mom, I'm sure Devon is busy."

Once again, Devon pulled herself back to the present, hoping she hadn't offended Cole by being so obviously surprised by the fact that he was an artist, one who was going to take part in the Arts and Crafts Trail.

"Maybe after the trail's opening weekend, I'll leave the shop in Mandy's hands and drive it myself. It'd be good to be familiar with all the stops in case anyone asks about specifics."

What would Cole look like working on a sculpture? Every time she'd thought of him in the years since high school, his image was always attached to rodeo and bulls. She imagined him with a welding iron, shaping pieces of metal to his will, sweat drenching his body to the point that he had to remove his shirt.

Ahhh, she couldn't think like that. She had to get out of there before she said or did something monumentally stupid and embarrassing. A glance at the smile on Barbara's face made Devon wonder if the older woman had some idea the route Devon's thoughts had been traveling. Forget about embarrassing. More like mortifying.

When Ryan Teague stopped to speak to Cole and Barbara, Devon made for the exit as if the back of her pants were on fire.

She was already a few steps out the front door when she stopped. Because she'd evidently ticked off fate today, her mother was walking straight toward her and it was too late to make an escape. When Devon spotted the nice-looking man in an impeccable suit accompanying her mother, a sinking feeling appeared and immediately dropped to the bottom of Devon's stomach.

"Devon, there you are, dear," her mother said, too bright and cheery. Devon wondered if anyone besides her could tell that it was a facade. "I think something's wrong with your phone. I tried to call you earlier. I thought you'd want to know so you can check on it."

Her mother knew good and well Devon had most likely ignored the call, but this was all a show for the man beside her. He might be a perfectly nice guy, but the mere fact that Devon knew what was coming soured her on him. Not to mention he didn't look at all like the kind of man she found attractive. His blond, perfect, high-end-magazine-ad appearance didn't fit in here in Blue Falls, and he certainly wasn't a good fit for Devon.

Not like Cole.

Stop thinking about him, especially in front of your mother.

Devon wasn't entirely sure her mother didn't have the ability to read minds. Angela Newberry just chose to ignore what she found there.

Her mother gave Devon's outfit—white drawstring cotton pants with pale orange pinstripes and a billowy orange peasant blouse—a disdainful look that her companion couldn't see.

"Sweetheart," Angela said, pouring on the mother-daughter closeness act a little thick, "I didn't want you to miss the opportunity to meet Steven Jackson. He's an attorney for one of your father's important customers, in town only for today. I told him he simply couldn't leave Blue Falls without exploring the charm of our fair town."

Devon resisted the urge to strangle her mother, instead deciding to beat her at her own game.

"I wouldn't dream of denying you that opportunity, Mom. After all, you know more about the town than I do since you've lived here longer."

The slight narrowing of her mother's eyes told Devon she was going to pay for that comment later when Steven Jackson was nowhere near to hear it. Still, her mother didn't listen to reason. She simply refused to believe that Devon didn't like any of the men her mother deemed appropriate for the only daughter of one of the county's wealthiest families.

"I can't, dear," her mother said. "I have a meeting that was planned before I knew Steven would be here."

Yeah, right.

"If it's an inconvenience, please don't worry about it," Steven said.

Before Devon could respond, her mother said, "Oh, nonsense. I'm sure Devon is free and would love to be your tour guide. I just heard that they have a new chef at the Wildflower Inn, too. You'll have to try it out and let me know how the food is."

Devon wouldn't be the least bit surprised if poor in-the-middle Steven could see the steam coming out of her ears.

"There you are, sweetie. Sorry we got held up in there."

Devon turned to Barbara, who'd stepped up beside her. Cole had to be close by, but Devon didn't look for him. She wasn't willing to risk that certain rush of heat up her neck and into her face in front of her mother.

"You ready to go?" Barbara asked Devon.

She was about to ask Barbara what in the world she was talking about when she realized the older woman was throwing her a lifeline. It didn't matter why, Devon decided to look at it as a gift from the universe and roll with it.

"Yes."

She could almost feel the anger radiating off her mother.

"Excuse us, Barbara, but Devon was making plans with Steven."

Devon barely kept herself from telling her mother she was being rude. How could anyone be rude to Barbara Davis? She was as sweet as pie.

"Devon already has plans to have dinner with us," Barbara responded. Was that a little edge to her voice? What was going on here?

Her mother's expression revealed a moment of shock, over in less than a blink when she pasted on her fake smile. "Perhaps you can reschedule. Steven is only in town from Dallas for this evening."

Steven looked like he wanted to be snatched up by a giant eagle and carried right out of this really uncomfortable situation. Devon didn't blame him.

Devon sensed movement on her left a moment before someone wrapped an arm around her shoulders.

Not someone. Cole.

She stiffened, afraid that if she moved he would disappear, taking his delicious warmth and fresh, clean, honest scent with him.

"You ready for dinner?" he asked. "I'm starving."

She was starving, all right. Starving for air. Starving for a regular heartbeat. Starving for the ability to be able to look up into his eyes without revealing just how much his simple gesture was rocking her world.

Chapter Two

When Cole wrapped his arm around Devon's shoulders, she went stiff as a fence post. He wondered if he'd made a miscalculation of how she'd respond, but then she relaxed a fraction and played along with the tale he and his mother were spinning by the seat of their pants.

Though he suspected his mother was up to something, he followed her lead. It was that or continuing to watch Devon's mother bully her. How the older woman was treating her daughter raised his ire, the same way he was angered anytime he saw a parent belittling or mistreating a child. He'd damn near gotten himself thrown in jail up in Wyoming the time he'd intervened when he'd seen a woman grab her little girl by her ponytail and nearly drag her out of a restaurant. Thankfully, there had been enough witnesses who took his side that he'd avoided ending up behind bars. But he wouldn't have done anything differently even if he had ended up there.

Granted, Devon was a grown woman, but that didn't suddenly give her mother the right to embarrass her in public.

"It was nice to meet you, Steven," Devon said, sounding sincere. "I hope you enjoy your visit to Blue Falls."

"Thank you," the man beside Angela Newberry said.

Cole fought the strange urge to dislike the guy, but it appeared Steven had been roped into this awkward situation unknowingly.

Angela appeared as though she was about to protest again, so Cole steered Devon away from her mother and toward the parking lot. Yes, it was partly to prevent Devon from having to endure any more pressure from her mother, but it was more so he'd remove himself from Angela's presence before he said something that would embarrass both his mom and Devon.

"Devon," Angela called out.

"'Bye, Mom." Devon threw a wave over her shoulder without looking back.

As they put distance between themselves and Angela, Devon didn't move to extricate herself from him. Most likely it was because she knew her mother was probably staring at Devon's back, but it felt good to have his arm wrapped around a woman again nonetheless.

Oh hell, he was not going there. If he could be sure Angela wasn't watching them, he'd be the first to step away. The absolute last thing he needed in his life was a woman. He'd been down that path more than once, and it always ended up dead-ending in Craptown.

When they maneuvered their way to the other side of his truck, he lifted his arm away from her and let it fall to his side while he propped his other arm along the side of his truck bed.

"Thanks for the rescue," Devon said, not making eye contact.

He wondered if she was embarrassed because he'd witnessed the disagreement between her and her mother or if it was that she'd allowed him to pose as something he wasn't. And would never be. He might convince himself to go on the occasional date, but from now on it was going to be casual one-and-done for him. Getting serious with someone led to marriage, and he'd tried that twice already and neither had ended well. There was no third-time's-the-charm.

"No problem," he said.

She shifted from one foot to the other, as if she might be about to turn and leave.

"You'll need to come out to the house now," his mom said as she joined them.

At that, Devon looked up.

"If you don't, your mom will find out and know this was all a ruse. Plus, it'd be nice to visit anyway. And you could see Cole's sculptures."

There it was, his mother's undying belief that "the one" was still out there for him, the woman who would love him and give his mom grandchildren. He could tell her a million times that he was done with marriage and she still refused to believe him.

"Neither of those marriages worked out because neither of them was the right woman," she'd said on more than one occasion.

He'd finally stopped wasting his breath. She'd figure it out when year after year passed by with him still single and childless. Leave it to his younger brother, Cooper, to be the provider of grandchildren. Maybe then his mom would abandon her determined hope for Cole's happily-ever-after.

He expected Devon to decline. Instead, she nodded.

"You're probably right. I hate that you all got sucked into the gravitational pull that is my mother's belief she can find the perfect man for me."

His mom made a dismissive sound. "Don't worry about it. We were happy to help."

In fact, his mom sounded a bit too happy. And for a

moment, Cole wasn't sure if all that barely contained glee was solely because she might have some match-making up her sleeve. Now that he thought about it, he remembered the occasional offhand remark from his mom about Angela Newberry that indicated she didn't like the other woman. He hadn't thought about it much when she'd made those remarks, but now he wondered if there was some bigger story there.

His mom clapped her hands together once. "Well, we better get going before Angela gets suspicious."

If Devon's mom had a lick of sense, she was already suspicious. But he guessed they had to run with this a while longer. As he slipped into the driver's seat of his truck, he couldn't help but glance toward where Devon was walking to her car. There was no denying she was pretty with that head full of long, curly red hair. And despite the fact that she lived in Texas, her skin wasn't tanned. Maybe with her fair complexion she burned easily and took caution in the sun.

"She's certainly grown into a beautiful woman, hasn't she?"

He shifted his attention to his mom sitting in the passenger seat. "You can just stop right there."

"What? I can't say when I think someone's pretty?"

He snorted. "We both know where you're going with this, and my view on the whole idea hasn't changed."

His mom sighed. "Fine. Maybe you two can at least be friends. With a mom like hers, I'm sure she could use them."

"What's up with you and Angela Newberry anyway?"

"She's always been too snooty for words, thinks she's better than everyone else."

He still thought there might be more to the story, but

he also knew when his mom wasn't going to say more on the subject. "Good enough reason for me."

He started the truck and pulled out onto Main Street, not allowing himself to check the rearview mirror to see if a certain redhead was following.

DEVON SHOOK HER head as she followed Cole and Barbara toward their ranch. Perhaps going through with the visit was overkill, but sometimes it felt as if her mother had eyes and ears everywhere. Not for the first time, Devon wondered how her life would be different if she'd moved away from Blue Falls, hundreds or even thousands of miles away from her family.

No doubt her mom would still find a way to know everything she was doing and criticize it. To Angela Newberry, Devon had chosen a life beneath her. She was supposed to marry a man with the right pedigree according to her mom, take part in carefully chosen causes and pop out a few babies while her husband was brought into the fold at Diamond Ranch Western Wear.

Ugh. The image made her skin crawl. It wasn't that the thought of marrying and having children repulsed her. But, funny thing, she'd like to be the one picking the husband in that scenario, preferably someone who looked at the world as she did, who wasn't bedazzled by her parents' money. Even the name of her parents' huge ranch and the namesake clothing company that produced high-end Western wear for everyone from governors to famous country singers didn't sit well with her. It sounded pretentious. She hated pretentious.

She much preferred her little sustainable farm, where she raised chickens, goats and sheep, spun wool, made goat's-milk soap. It provided the peace and freedom from stress that she'd lacked growing up. Money often couldn't buy you the things you wanted most. She'd even chosen a simple name for her home, Phlox Farm, because the hillside next to her house had been covered in bright purple phlox the first time she'd seen it. So unlike Diamond Ranch, where the only diamonds to be found were on her mother's hand or in her jewelry box.

The day she'd visited her farm, it had been love at first sight. When her mother had found out where Devon was moving, she'd sworn Devon had lost her mind. Her mom didn't realize that by saying that, it only made Devon more convinced she'd done the right thing by buying it.

She lifted her hand to shade the setting sun trying to blind her through the driver's-side window. Leaving thoughts of the past in the past where they belonged, she focused on the pickup in front of her, and not getting so lost in her memories that she drove too close to it.

Cole looked over toward his mom, putting his strong profile on display. Devon's heartbeat did a disconcerting fluttery thing, causing her to take a slow, deep breath to calm the rhythm. She had to purge this problematic attraction, especially if she didn't want to trip over her own tongue and make an idiot of herself while she had to spend time at the ranch.

She nearly hit the brakes and turned around. She'd ceased letting her mother have power over her decisions years ago, and yet here she was, willing to go hide out at the Davis ranch simply because her mom was trying to fix her up again.

This wasn't your idea.

No, but she hadn't put the kibosh on it, either.

Good grief, she was putting too much importance on the impending visit. She liked Barbara, who was friendly and a faithful customer of the fabric section of

A Good Yarn. Both she and Cole had helped her out, so
the least she could do was maybe have a cup of coffee
with them, take a gander at Cole's work, say some ap-
propriately complimentary words, then head home to
that bath and book that seemed to keep getting further
and further away.

Several miles north of town, Cole finally put on his
left-turn signal and pulled into his family's ranch. She
wondered what it had felt like to him when he'd returned
home after several years on the rodeo circuit. When he'd
left right after high school, his father had been alive and
his younger brother had still been at home. Now it was
Cooper out riding the circuit, so Cole had come home
to only his mom.

Devon's heart went out to Barbara. She couldn't
imagine what it must have been like for her to lose the
man she'd loved for so long, to suddenly be alone on
a ranch that used to be filled with her family. Though
Devon had never seen Barbara being anything other
than smiling and quick with a kind word, there had to
have been a lot of sad, dark, lonely days for her.

After they'd both parked, Devon hesitated a moment as Cole slid from his truck. She'd swear his jean-
encased legs had gotten longer in the time it had taken
to drive from town. Deciding she wasn't going to get
any less antsy sitting in her car, she got out and followed Barbara into the house, trying not to think about
Cole behind her.

She almost snorted at herself. What was there to
be worried about? It wasn't as if he was checking out
her curves. She wasn't a fan of clothing that clung
too tightly. Plus, didn't guys love gorgeous blondes or
long, leggy brunettes, and not someone who looked like

she was the hair twin of a certain flame-haired, bow-wielding princess?

The moment she stepped inside the house, a gray, long-haired cat nuzzled against her legs.

"Looks like you already have Jasper's seal of approval," Barbara said.

Devon knelt and petted the cat, causing him to begin purring so loudly she laughed a little. "You've got quite the motor running, Jasper."

"He thinks you'll give him treats if he does that," Cole said as he walked past her. "I wonder where he gets that idea."

Devon looked up in time to see Cole give his mom a pointed look.

"I admit I spoil him, and I'm not sorry. Besides, you're the one who gave him to me. You're complicit."

Devon smiled at their banter, but a part of her heart ached that she couldn't have this with her mom. She loved her mother, but it was so difficult to be around her. But from her mother's point of view, she wasn't at fault for that fact. So Devon kept her distance as best she could and tried not to think about the tiny ember of hope that still burned deep inside her that one day her mom would chill out some and they could have a real, nonadversarial relationship.

"Come on in the kitchen, hon," Barbara said, making a motion for Devon to follow her. "I just made some lemon squares earlier. Would you like one while I make dinner?"

"I'll hold off for now, thanks. And you don't have to feed me. I can just stay for a few minutes, then head out."

"Nonsense. You already drove all the way out here. Might as well stay and eat. It'll be nice to have company for dinner. I think Cole gets tired just staring at my mug at every meal."

"I doubt that."

"Regardless, please say you'll stay."

Devon hesitated for a moment, then said, "Okay, but tell me what I can do to help."

She ended up cutting thick slices of homemade sourdough bread as Barbara prepared fresh chicken salad. Despite Devon's hyperawareness of Cole on the other side of the room pulling dishes from cabinets and setting the table, her mouth watered at the thought of the upcoming sandwich. She hadn't eaten much for lunch, and the homemade food looked delicious.

"I'm sorry we don't have anything more substantial," Barbara said as she removed a jar of pickles—likely canned from her garden—from the fridge. Next came a container of potato salad, also homemade.

"Are you kidding? This all looks wonderful."

Barbara chuckled. "You, my dear, are easy to please."

Devon didn't miss the quick glance Barbara sent her son's way. Barbara had given her an escape hatch from her mother's matchmaking attempt, but was she trying for the same thing, albeit with a lighter, kinder touch?

Devon's nerves ratcheted up a notch when they all sat down at the table and she found herself across from Cole. She had three choices: keep Barbara engaged in conversation throughout the entirety of the meal, focus her attention on her plate or risk being lured into Cole's blue-eyed gaze.

"So, how's your store doing?" Barbara asked.

Good, a safe topic.

"Really well, thankfully. I'm coming up on the two-year anniversary of my opening, so I'm thinking about having some sort of special event."

"Sounds like a good idea." Barbara turned her attention to Cole. "Did I tell you that Devon has her own farm where she raises goats and sheep?"

"You might have mentioned it."

The way he said it made Devon wonder if Barbara had talked about her with Cole more than once. Though that thought was unnerving, she didn't mind it in the way she did her mother's persistent meddling. Maybe because she suspected that Barbara would stop any futile attempts at matchmaking if Devon asked her to.

"What do you do with the animals?" Cole asked.

That he actually sounded interested surprised her. "I use the wool to make yarn, which I color with natural dyes and put in my shop. I use the milk from the goats to make soap."

"That stuff is a miracle for my skin," Barbara said as she smoothed her fingertips over the back of the opposite hand.

"Sounds like you enjoy it," Cole said to Devon.

She did, and it touched her that he was able to pick up on that. "I do, much to my mother's chagrin."

Now, why had she said that? Hadn't they been witness to enough of her mother's disdain already?

"We all have to follow our own paths," Barbara said. "Would I have chosen a career for both of my boys that took them far away from home for months at a time and put them in danger? Probably not. But I know how much it meant to them, same as your farm and shop do to you." Barbara patted Devon's hand where it rested beside her plate.

An unexpected lump formed in Devon's throat. How lucky Cole and Cooper were to grow up with such a mother. They might not have been wealthy, but they'd been rich in the ways that mattered most.

The three of them fell into a conversation about all the changes in Blue Falls over the past few years and specifically about the Arts and Crafts Trail as they finished up their dinner.

"Cole, show Devon what you're working on," Barbara said.

Cole looked across the table at Devon, and she wondered how many women had fallen for that face, those eyes. Who could blame them?

"Are you interested?" he asked, his tone making it sound as if he'd be surprised if she said yes.

"Yeah. I'll admit to being curious."

"Excellent," Barbara said. "You two go on. I'll take care of all this." She gestured toward the dirty dishes.

"Let me help," Devon said.

"Nah, I'll have this done by the time you reach the barn."

Devon didn't feel she could argue more or her nervousness about being alone with Cole might become obvious. Why had she agreed to look at his sculptures? Oh yeah, she really was curious.

She smiled when Cole held the door open for her, unable to prevent the thought that he looked even more scrumptious when he was being chivalrous. But as they walked side by side toward the barn, she told herself to stop thinking that way. What was the use? What she could do was think of him as a friend. It would probably be nice to have Cole Davis as a friend. And really, who couldn't use more friends?

"Sorry if you feel we roped you into more than you bargained for," Cole said.

"No, not at all. I was thankful for the life preserver."

As he opened the barn door, the look on his face made him appear as if he wanted to say something else.

Devon stopped and faced him. "What?"

"Is your mom that…persistent all the time?"

"In a word, yes."

"I'm sorry."

His apology, when he'd done nothing wrong, took her aback. But then it clicked that he was simply sorry she had to deal with that kind of pressure.

She shrugged. "Nothing new." She pointed inside. "So, let's see these sculptures your mom has been raving about like you're the Michelangelo of Blue Falls."

Cole snorted as he accompanied her inside. He flicked on the overhead lights as they walked into the barn. The first thing she saw was a beautiful roan horse that looked their way with large, dark eyes, a reminder that this was a working ranch even if Cole dabbled in art as a hobby.

"Who's this handsome fella?" she asked as she approached the stall and rubbed along the silky smoothness of the horse's jaw. It was obvious at a glance that Cole took good care of his horses.

"This here's Duncan." He scratched the horse between the ears.

"Duncan?"

"Named after Duncan, Oklahoma, where I won my first pro rodeo."

"Ah. Well, it's nice to meet you, Duncan."

The horse sniffed at her hand then rubbed his head against her.

"He's a big flirt," Cole said.

"I can see that."

"Come on." Cole motioned for her to follow him. "My work area is back here."

Devon did her best not to admire Cole's physical attributes as she followed him to the back corner of the barn, where he'd knocked out the dividers between a few stalls to create a bigger space. In the middle of that space was a sculpture of a rearing horse, mane flying. It took a second look for her to realize that the whole was made up of many pieces that used to be parts of other things.

She stepped up close and slowly made her way around the horse. An old, rusty, metal tractor seat, chains, a muffler, truck rims and countless pieces she couldn't identify shouldn't be able to come together to make something so beautiful, but they did.

"It's stunning," she said, in awe of the obvious talent she would have never thought to attribute to Cole.

"That's overstating it a bit."

She shifted her gaze from the horse to Cole. "No, it's not. Not everyone could do this. Heck, not everyone could even think this. If I were to see this stuff separately, there's no way I could imagine how to put it all together to come up with something like this."

Cole leaned against the side of the stall and crossed his arms, showcasing just how incredibly nice and tanned and strong those arms were. Yeah, she might have a thing for men's arms.

"Well, we must be two really talented individuals then because my idea of soap is grabbing it at the grocery store."

She shuddered, making him laugh. Her heart filled with puppies and rainbows and sparkly unicorns. Why did he have to have a sexy laugh, too? Didn't he know she was trying to be friends, nothing more? Of course, he didn't.

Devon shushed the conversation going on in her head and turned to look at some smaller finished pieces that sat along the back wall. A small bison, a cowboy sitting on a fence, even a starfish. She pointed to the starfish.

"This one reminds me of that game, 'which of these is not like the others?'" She turned back toward him to see his expression dim for a moment.

"Reminds me of a vacation we had when Cooper and I were kids. Only time we went to the beach. I remember walking along holding my dad's hand and we found a starfish. Mom still has a picture of me squatting down in the sand next to it with the goofiest grin on my face."

Devon smiled at the image in her mind. "How did you get started doing this?"

"Would you believe rodeo?"

She turned more fully toward him. "Not connecting the dots here."

He pushed away from the side of the stall and propped his hand atop one of the posts. "I was riding in a rodeo up in Wyoming and had some time to kill. Went to a local museum, and they had this kind of sculpture out front. A whole herd of bison. I thought it was neat, and the idea stuck with me. When I retired, I thought I'd give it a try in my spare time."

She wondered if he was using the sculpture work to fill a void. "I was surprised when I heard you retired. You seemed like you really loved riding bulls, though personally I think it's insane."

Cole laughed. "You and my mom, both." He shifted his gaze to the metal horse. "It wasn't by choice. But my old body couldn't take it anymore."

His old body? From what she could tell, his body was perfectly fine. More than fine. Superfine.

Oh, stop it.

He appeared to notice her confusion. "Was thrown too many times. Doc told me that if I didn't want to risk being paralyzed the next time I hit the dirt, I'd better hang it up."

Sickness coiled in Devon's stomach at the image of Cole in a wheelchair. For a man like him, it might kill him. At least kill the person he was, how he identified himself.

"I'm sorry. That sucks."

"Yes. Yes, it does." He stepped forward and rapped his knuckles against the metal horse's neck. "But I stay busy so I won't think about how I thought I had a few more good years of riding in me."

"I'm going to go out on a limb and say that doesn't work as often as you'd like."

He looked at her with a surprised expression, eyes slightly wider, then gave a single nod. "But at least I'm still walking, right?"

She could tell he was making light of the situation when probably, deep down, he hadn't fully come to terms with it yet. She couldn't imagine how broken-hearted she'd be if she were to lose the farm and the shop. But they weren't the type of friends who bared all their emotions to each other. At least not yet. Maybe not ever.

"Yay for mobility. Allows us to run away from our matchmaking mamas." As soon as she said it, she wished she could rewind time a few seconds.

But Cole laughed. "You picked up on Mom's intent, huh? Sorry about that. She's got a hankering for grand-kids and hasn't accepted that she's not going to get them from me."

His words caused a sadness to settle on Devon. Not that she thought the two of them were going to make babies or anything, but he seemed so certain. His assertion had a finality to it that didn't invite argument.

It seemed a shame not to carry on his family line and those magnificent genes.

"You don't like kids?"

He shrugged. "They're fine, but I'm never getting married again. And if I had kids, I'd want to be around for them, not part of a broken family. I'd want them to have what I did growing up."

She envied his fond thoughts of childhood. When she looked back, what overwhelmed her were feelings of inadequacy and trying to find ways to make herself feel better and less alone.

Devon resisted the urge to ask about Amy, what had happened. She didn't even know his second wife's name. Maybe Cole was right to steer clear of marriage after that track record, but something about that thought didn't sit well with her. She didn't have any real basis other than he seemed to be a nice guy and loved his mom, but Devon thought Cole Davis might make someone a good husband. But the right someone.

Like you?

No, not me.

She'd learned long ago not to expect things that would never come to fruition. Doing so only led to sadness and burning frustration.

"What about you?" he asked. "Are you anti-marriage or just anti-marrying someone your mother picks?"

"The latter. Honestly, I sometimes feel like she's set up a dating profile for me somewhere and carefully screens all the candidates before attempting to parade me in front of them like a prize cow."

Cole snort-laughed.

"You laugh, but I'm not exaggerating. At least your mom is sweet about her attempts."

"Sounds like we could each use someone watching our backs."

"I like how you think."

"So you encourage my mom to chill on trying to find me wife number three, and I'll play fake date when you need to get your mom off your case."

Devon resisted gulping at the idea of a pretend date with Cole. Would she be able to hide the fact that she really found him attractive? That she wouldn't mind if the date were real?

"You are so getting the worst end of this deal," she said.

Chapter Three

After Devon left, Cole stayed in the barn to continue working on the horse sculpture. He'd been so busy on the ranch the past few days that he hadn't found time to come out here. With Devon's enthusiastic reaction, he found himself energized and picked up an old metal sign and began bending it to cover a part of the horse's flank.

His thoughts drifted back to Devon. Though she attempted to joke about it, his gut told him that her mother's treatment of her was no laughing matter. Angela Newberry was the type of woman who was used to getting what she wanted and didn't react well when she didn't. He'd had experience with that type and couldn't say he liked it a whole hell of a lot.

He tried to pull up memories of Devon from high school. She'd been smart, shy, maybe heavier, but he couldn't remember all the details. It struck him that despite their school's small size, she'd still managed to be one of the kids you tended to overlook. Despite who her parents were, she hadn't ruled the school as you'd expect someone in her position to do. He wondered if even then her mother was always harping on her.

She was thinner now, very pretty in a natural way. He found he liked that a lot better than the endless parade of overly made-up fakes who'd put themselves in his path. Not that Devon was doing that. In fact, he and his mother were the ones who'd dragged her out here. He was surprised by how nice it felt to be able to talk with a woman without feeling as though she expected something from him, like a ring on her finger. That Devon seemed to understand how he missed rodeo and appreciated his work made him extra glad he'd gone on instinct helping her with her mom earlier.

"You sound happy."

He looked up at his mom striding down the middle of the barn. "Huh?"

"You were whistling."

He was?

He placed his palm against the side of the metal horse. "Because I'm close to finishing this guy."

"You sure it has nothing to do with our visitor?"

"Devon?"

She lifted a brow. "You see any other visitors out here tonight?"

"Saw a couple of deer up the hill a few minutes ago."

She huffed out a sigh.

"Don't sound so put out. We were helping your friend out of a bad situation, nothing more."

"But she's a lovely, sweet girl."

"I'm sure she is, but I've told you I'm done."

"You're only thirty-three. That's awfully young to be giving up, isn't it?"

"Not from my perspective. You keep getting burned, you stop touching the stove."

"Cole—"

He held up a hand to stop her. "Mom, just because you found happiness in marriage doesn't mean everyone will. And I'm happy," he said, because he knew that was her chief worry despite her comments about wanting grandchildren. "I'm back home ranching. I've found something else I like to do. I get to eat my mom's home cooking every day. What's not to like?"

He'd swear he saw his mom deflate a bit, like a balloon slowly losing air. He felt bad about it, but he had to stand firm or she wouldn't quit her futile quest to find his one true love.

"Just keep an open mind, okay?"

He didn't respond, knowing it would be a lie if he agreed.

"How about you answer a question for me?" he said. "What's really up with you and Angela Newberry?"

"I don't like snobs."

"I know. But there's more to it."

"You're Sherlock Holmes all of a sudden?"

"Maybe."

His mom chuckled at that.

He let it go because he knew continuing to question his mom would be about as productive as digging a well with a measuring cup.

When his mom finally went back to the house after watching him work for a few minutes, her efforts to fix him up marched around inside his head again. Yes, Devon was nice. And she was pretty. But he'd proved he and marriage just weren't cut out for each other. And dating someone in Blue Falls if you didn't hope it led to a lifetime commitment just didn't seem wise. If it ended badly—and his track record indicated it would— he couldn't avoid seeing another Blue Falls resident the rest of his life.

So pursuing Devon? A big no-no. No matter how nice she was. Or how pretty.

DESPITE HOW TIRED she'd been when she arrived home the night before, Devon didn't sleep particularly well. She kept thinking about her mother's complete lack of respect for her as a person one minute and the warm, masculine feel of Cole's arm around her shoulders the next. No matter how many times she told herself that they could only be friends, and that she should count herself lucky with that much, she couldn't help the zing that just thinking about him caused.

Thankfully, Mandy was opening the store this morning, which gave Devon time to finish packaging a fresh supply of soap and stop by the Mehlerhaus Bakery for a cheese Danish and the biggest cup of coffee they had.

"Someone appears to need a lot of caffeine this morning," Josephina Mehler said as she handed over the coffee.

"It's one of those mornings where I feel like I need to swim through an ocean of coffee to get going."

Josephina laughed. "I know that feeling."

Work at a bakery started early. Josephina and her sister-in-law, Keri Teague, who owned the bakery, were probably the first people into downtown each morning.

She waved a goodbye and headed for the door, pausing when Talia Monroe stepped inside with her stepdaughter, Mia.

"Good morning," Devon said. "How are you all?"

Talia smiled and placed her hand lovingly on Mia's head. "Great, actually. We're here for celebratory sweets. Miss Mia just had her latest checkup and got another clean bill of health."

"Cancer-free!" Mia said with great exuberance as she threw her arms out wide.

"That's awesome." Devon leaned down to meet Mia's gaze. "That is a great reason for a treat."

An idea popped into her head, something she could do during her anniversary celebration.

"Mia, I have an idea for something to do at my store, and I was wondering if you'd give me your opinion."

"Sure." Mia crossed her arms, and her expression changed from gleeful, cancer-free kid to serious consideration, like she was a mini adult.

"Do you think kids like you would be interested in learning how to knit? We could do fun things that you could give as Christmas gifts." She was making it up on the fly, but the more she said, the more she liked the idea.

"Sounds cool." She looked up at Talia. "Could I do that?"

"I don't see why not." Talia met Devon's gaze as Devon stood to her full height again. "Great idea."

After insisting on buying Mia's and Talia's pastries, Devon headed to the shop feeling really good. Nothing like a jolt of coffee and learning that a sweet little girl was healthy after her struggle with the big, dreaded *C* word to put pep in your step. She was darn near skipping by the time she stepped into the shop.

"Good morning, Mandy," she said in greeting to her best friend since the second grade.

Devon barely had time to detect the tense look of warning on Mandy's face before she saw movement out of the corner of her eye. Devon knew before turning that it was her mother. It was something about how the air changed near her, as if it crackled before a lightning strike.

"We need to talk about your rude behavior," her mom said without any preamble.

"Good morning to you, too, Mom." Devon rounded the front counter and stuffed her purse underneath it in the safe alongside Mandy's.

"Don't be smart with me."

"If you're here about your sneak attack on me yesterday, you can save your breath."

"Attack? That's what you call my having your best interests in mind when I introduce you to a handsome, successful young man?" Angela shifted her attention to Mandy. "Dear, don't you have somewhere else you can be?"

"I work here, remember?"

Devon bit her lip, trying not to laugh. In the past, her mother had first scared Mandy, then hurt her feelings. The fact that Mandy hadn't had much money growing up, had been the daughter of a single mother who had to work three jobs to make ends meet, had made her an inappropriate friend for Devon, according to her mother.

"Your father and I have an image to uphold. It's what your father's customers expect," she'd said when Devon was only nine. "Some people just don't fit into our world."

Our world. Even at that young age, Devon had known her mother was a snob. And despite the fact that her mother scared her, too, Devon had refused to stop being friends with Mandy. In fact, they'd become inseparable. When Devon had reached high school, her mother had blamed Mandy for Devon's lack of popularity. The woman hadn't been able to see that she was the reason. She'd driven her only daughter into a self-protective shell built from books, crafts, baggy clothes and lots of comfort food.

Her mother looked exasperated as she shifted her piercing gaze back to Devon. "You embarrassed me yesterday. I had to try to explain away your rudeness."

"I wasn't rude. I was perfectly cordial to Steven because I figured he got dragged into the situation with no clue about the backstory." Devon braced her palms against the top of the counter. "I've told you over and over to stop trying to fix me up with these men you deem appropriate. I'm not interested."

"Which just proves that you don't know what's best for you. I mean, seriously, Cole Davis? Please tell me you're not dating him."

Devon detected a barely contained sound of shock from Mandy. She'd have to explain everything when her mom finally vacated the premises.

"There's nothing wrong with Cole."

"He has nothing to offer you."

"At least he isn't trying to make me something I'm not."

Her mother opened her mouth to speak again, but she instantly transformed her expression to one of perfectly crafted cordiality when the mayor came through the front door.

But before her mother could say anything, Devon beat her to it. "Good morning, Karen."

Mayor Karen Tompkins smiled. "Good morning."

Devon noticed the way her mother's expression shifted back to one that promised another scolding, but Devon chose to ignore her, at least for the moment.

"What can I help you with?"

Karen pointed toward the large candles. "I need something that will make my office smell like anything other than the plumbing work they're finally doing."

After Devon helped Karen select a large lemon-scented candle and accepted her payment, the mayor hurried off to make an early meeting with several other mayors from throughout the Hill Country.

"You do realize it's appropriate to address Mayor Tompkins by her title?" Angela said the moment the front door closed behind Karen.

It was the last straw. Devon rounded on her mother. "And you do realize that I'm not a child who has to live under your overbearing thumb anymore, right?"

Devon suspected she should feel ashamed of talking to her mother in such a way, but she didn't. In fact, seeing the anger burning in her mother's eyes gave her a sense of empowerment that didn't often make an appearance when she was around her mom.

"Mark my words. You will regret talking to me this way when you want my help. You'll realize that you've made a lot of mistakes and that I've been right all along."

"I doubt that."

"Remember you said that when your choices lead to failure and heartbreak."

Devon started to make a retort, feeling like she was on a roll, but her mother lifted her hand to stop her.

"If nothing else, at least find someone who isn't so…" Her mom made a face, as if she thought Cole might smell like horse manure.

"What, Mom? Beneath me?" Well, that brought up an interesting image in her head, one she simply could not indulge while facing her mother. "Cole is a good man, and you're just going to have to get used to seeing us together."

Her mother shook her head and strode out of the shop without another word. Devon wasn't fooled into thinking her mother had suddenly given up, though.

She also wasn't fooled that her mom's displeasure with Devon's choices had much to do with Devon at all. No, her mother was more worried about how those choices reflected on her and the precious family name. Sometimes Devon wondered if her mom thought she was royalty and shouldn't mix with the commoners.

Devon sank onto a tall stool behind the counter, already exhausted and the day had barely started. A few ticks of the clock on the wall behind her went by before she noticed that Mandy was staring at her with her mouth slightly parted.

"You're dating Cole Davis? How exactly did that happen? And why didn't you tell me?" The pitch of Mandy's voice went up with each question.

Devon shook her head. "I'm not really dating Cole."

"But…you just told your mother that you were. How long do you think it's going to take before that gets around?"

"After her objections, do you really think she'd start spouting it to everyone on Main Street?"

"No, but I can see her cornering Cole and telling him to stay away from you because you're destined to be the wife of a future governor or something."

The sinking feeling in Devon's stomach was almost audible.

"And how in the world did she get this idea in the first place?" Mandy asked.

Trying to quell the feeling that she'd just taken a nosedive into quicksand, Devon recounted what had happened the previous evening at the meeting and then out at the Davis ranch.

"Dang," Mandy said when she was finished, sounding disappointed.

"What's that mean?"

"I was hoping maybe you were actually sneaking around with Cole. That dude is hotter than a grill on the Fourth of July."

Devon couldn't disagree, but she shook her head at the idea of them dating. "And us actually being a couple is about as likely as igloos being built next to that grill."

"Why do you say that?"

"Isn't that obvious?"

"No, it isn't."

"Mandy—"

"Don't *Mandy* me. You're smart, successful, fun, beautiful."

"I appreciate the best-friend pep talk, but it doesn't help me out of this mess I've obviously made."

I'll play fake date when you need to get your mom off your case.

Cole's words echoed in her head. Had he really meant it, or was he just joking around? Would he maybe agree to fake it for just long enough for her mom to get wrapped up in some project that would give Devon some peace for a while? Could *she* fake it without letting him know that she really did find him incredibly attractive?

But her mother's insistence that she knew what was best for Devon ate at her, driving her toward doing something she'd normally never do. As a rule, she despised lying, but nothing she said or did ever seemed to make a dent in her mother's determination to run Devon's life for her.

"What's that expression?" Mandy asked. "It feels like I'm watching a plan come together."

"I need to make a phone call." Before she could chicken out, Devon grabbed her cell from her purse and hurried to the storeroom, ignoring Mandy's parade of questions.

Once she stepped behind the curtain that hid the storage room from the rest of the store, her hands shook so much that she nearly dropped her phone. What she was considering was a totally crazy idea, right? She was sure to say or do something to give herself away. How could she possibly hide the fact that, yes, Cole Davis was indeed as hot as a grill on the Fourth of July? If that grill was on the face of the sun.

But was faking it a little while any worse than allowing her mother to know that she'd lied to her about Cole? She leaned back against the wall and brought her palm to her forehead. Why couldn't she have been like most kids who grew up with overbearing parents and moved far, far away once she was old enough? Why did she have to love Blue Falls and its people? Want to make her life here? Could fake-dating Cole for a while finally get her mother to stop meddling in her life?

Only one way to find out. She took a deep breath and started to dial Cole's number, only to realize she didn't have it. She could have taken that as a sign that her plan was a really bad idea. Instead, she remembered the list of trail participants she'd gotten the night before and how Gina had showed them how all the contact information for the artists and craftsmen was on a dedicated page of the Tourist Bureau's website. One quick search later, and she was looking at Cole's number.

Before she could talk herself out of it, she called Cole and almost hoped he wouldn't answer. Instead, he picked up on the second ring.

"Hello?" Cole said a second time, with that decrease in friendliness that said he thought perhaps it was a telemarketer on her end of the call.

"Oh, hey. It's Devon Newberry."

"Hey. What can I do for you?"

"Um, well, you remember how you said you'd…that you might be willing to go out on a fake date to help me out with my mom? Yeah, how serious were you about that?"

The hesitation on the other end of the call made Devon's stomach churn. Oh God, she'd made a horrible mistake, just as her mother had predicted.

No, she couldn't let her mom be right.

"I might be convinced to hang out if there was some pizza involved."

Devon couldn't help the relieved laugh that escaped her. "Buddy, I will buy you whatever kind and however many pizzas you want."

Chapter Four

Cole stood in front of his closet, wondering what he'd gotten himself into. This wasn't a real date, so no need to dress like it was. But to help Devon out with her mom, he needed to expend at least a little thought on what to wear so he didn't look like he'd arrived straight from working in the barn all day.

"Wear the blue one."

He looked toward his bedroom door to see his mom pointing toward his open closet.

"Don't get any ideas," he said. "We're just doing this so Angela will lay off Devon for a while."

"Hate to tell you, but I doubt Angela will stop trying to foist some fancy suit-wearing guy on Devon, even if you two convince her that you're really a couple. And if you're convincing enough, who's to say it might not become real?"

Again, why had he agreed to this? He needed Devon to fulfill her end of the bargain as well by telling his mom their "dating" was totally fake, that he truly had no interest in getting serious with anyone ever again. In hindsight, he realized he hadn't thought his offer through before opening his mouth. His deal with Devon would have worked better in a sizable city where they didn't know everyone in town and gossip hadn't been perfected to an art form.

He wore a green shirt, instead. One a couple of years old but still presentable. As best he could guess, it walked the line between not feeding the hopes his mom had of marrying him off again while also not embarrassing Devon.

And he was giving a damn shirt way too much thought.

After he finished dressing, he headed for the front door. His mom was sitting in the living room working on her latest quilt. When she looked up, she just shook her head. She didn't need to say what she was thinking—that he was being deliberately stubborn.

Reining in a grin, he walked over and dropped a kiss atop her head.

"Be back in a while," he said.

"Take your time."

He had too many things to do to spend too much time on this fake date. He suspected Devon did as well and probably resented having to spend the time and tell the lie her mother had forced her into. Despite his mom's tendency to try to fix him up, he realized he'd gotten darn lucky in the mom lottery. If he'd had a mother like Angela, he doubted he would have ever come back home. It made him wonder why Devon had stuck around Blue Falls. She could have started her business and had her farm in a million different places, and yet she'd stayed.

If he thought about it, maybe his leaving a family with whom he got along well made about as much sense.

When he reached Gia's Pizza in town, he spotted Devon sitting in a booth toward the back working on a tablet computer as she sipped on what looked like a glass of water. Should he have picked her up? Meeting here seemed more like friends getting together, which of course was more accurate even though he wasn't sure they were technically friends yet.

But if tonight was supposed to help convince her mother that they were dating, he should have picked her up, opened the door for her. Too late now. He'd just be sure to pay the check.

She looked up as he approached and smiled a little, almost as if she was uncomfortable. Before he had a chance to say anything, she spoke.

"Sorry about this," she said as she slid the tablet to the side.

"About what?"

"Pulling you into this mess."

He waved off her concern. "Don't worry about it. Doesn't take a lot of arm-twisting to get me to come eat some pizza."

She sat back against her side of the booth. "Figured you were more of a classic meat-and-potatoes kind of guy."

"Wouldn't argue with that either, but you get used to eating what's fast on the road. Burgers, fries, pizza."

"Heart attack waiting to happen."

"I think my mom agrees with you. I've noticed a lot of vegetables on my plate since I moved home."

"So you're King of the Green Bean now?"

"Among other things. Let's just say this will be a treat."

Devon lowered her gaze just as their teenage waitress slid menus in front of them.

"What kind of pizza do you like?" he asked Devon.

"Pretty much anything. I'd say no to anchovies, but

no need since I'm almost certain an anchovy has never crossed the city limits of Blue Falls."

"I'd say that's a safe bet."

When she insisted that she truly didn't care what kind of pizza they got, he went for a classic pepperoni.

When the waitress left, he leaned his forearms on the table. "So what did your mom do that prompted the quick call?"

"Showed up at my shop to chastise me for being rude to her and Steven."

"Pot, meet kettle."

"Exactly," she said as if relieved she'd finally found someone who understood where she was coming from.

"Has she always been on your case like this?"

Devon laced her fingers together atop the table, and for a moment he thought she might not answer.

"Unfortunately, yes. Not always about whom I should date, but there was always something."

He realized this was a bit of a heavy conversation for a first date, even if it was all an act. Still, it didn't seem forced at all.

"Why did you stay here?"

"In Blue Falls?"

He nodded.

"I've asked myself that I don't know how many times, but the short answer is that I love it here, always have, and I hated the idea of leaving my friends."

He thought she must really like the town and her friends to put up with her mother trying to run her life, but he didn't say it.

"I always thought you'd go off to a big city somewhere and do something like cure cancer or become a bestselling writer."

She looked at him as if he'd lost his mind.

"What would make you think I'd do either of those things?"

"You were so good at school, in every subject. Blowing the curves for everyone."

When Devon lowered her gaze to the tabletop, he realized how that must have sounded.

"Which wasn't your fault. The rest of us just should have studied more."

"It's okay. I don't mind that I was a bookworm. I still am. Being a nerd is cool now, don't you know?"

She said the words, but he wasn't sure there wasn't some hurt there anyway.

"Did your mom make you study a lot?"

"She expected good grades, but…let's just say that kids who aren't popular often retreat into books. It's our happy place."

It was a strange thought, her being unpopular while also being probably the wealthiest kid at their school. He guessed it shouldn't be so surprising. Some of the happiest people he'd ever met probably hadn't had ten bucks in their pocket. Still, the faded memories of her from high school—shy, withdrawn, bookish—made him wonder if she'd been unhappy. If books were her happy place, did that mean the real world was the opposite?

"I'm sorry if I was ever a jerk to you in school."

She looked up at him and shook her head. "You weren't. Can't say the same for your girlfriend, though."

As soon as the words left her mouth, Devon's eyes widened and her lips parted in surprise, as if she hadn't intended to voice her thoughts out loud.

"I'm sorry," she said. "That was rude."

"Not at all. In fact, I agree with you. I was just too stupid to realize it until about a year into our marriage.

I stuck it out another year, hoping in vain I hadn't been so wrong about her."

"What happened?"

"You mean besides the fact that once we left high school and she was no longer the center of attention, she couldn't handle it and blamed me?"

"Oh, ouch."

He shrugged. "We were young and dumb."

"Where is she now?"

"Last I heard, she was in California. Every time I see her mom in town, I do my best to steer clear."

"She's mad at you?"

"I'd rather not find out."

"Sounds like we both have locals we need to put GPS trackers on."

Cole laughed. "Not a bad idea. Maybe I'll put one on my mom while we're at it."

"But your mom is so sweet."

"And just as determined to find me a wife. Been down that road twice, not going to try for a third."

Devon nodded but didn't say anything. What was there to say? It was just nice to talk to a woman who actually understood where he was coming from. This whole fake-dating thing might be just what he needed. Who better to convince his mom that he was done with matrimony than a woman she liked and respected? One she obviously hoped he might make wife number three.

THERE WAS NO doubt in Cole's voice whatsoever when he said he was done with marriage. Despite the fact that this date wasn't real and Devon knew there was no future with someone like Cole, she couldn't help the feeling of sadness that filled her at his proclamation. Cole Davis seemed like a good guy, a hard worker, someone who took a hit to his life plan and forged a different path, not to mention he was as sexy as the summer solstice was long. The fact that he'd sworn off a chance at happily ever after at such a young age was a damn shame.

"So, what happened with your second wife?"

"It didn't work out."

The tightening of Cole's features and the way he looked away from her and across the restaurant told her this was one topic he wasn't interested in pursuing. Which of course made her intensely curious. But if he didn't want to talk about it, she'd respect that. There were certainly things in her life that she'd rather leave in the past, as well.

Their pizza arrived, momentarily interrupting their conversation. It distracted Cole long enough for her to hide any thoughts she might have had regarding him, her and a walk down the aisle. That was crazy anyway. Helping each other out was one thing. Letting herself imagine it turning into something deep and meaningful was quite another.

"What about you?" Cole asked as he pulled a large slice of pizza onto his plate. "You want to get married and have kids someday?"

"I'm not opposed to it, but Mr. Right hasn't come along yet." She would not wonder if Cole could turn into that Mr. Right. Hard to achieve a happily-ever-after when one of the parties didn't believe those existed. Not that he'd want to be with her even if he hadn't sworn off marriage.

"You believe in that kind of thing, that there's a Mr. Right out there for you?"

She shrugged. "Maybe, maybe not. At the moment, I'm more interested in this pizza and making sure my mom thinks our little farce is the beginning of a long and beautiful romance."

Devon made sure to smile and add some dramatic effect to her words so Cole wouldn't guess that at least part of her wouldn't mind seeing where a real relationship might take them.

The conversation veered away from their respective views on holy matrimony and into a discussion about what he was working on.

"It's amazing," she said, thinking of the look she'd gotten at the horse statue in progress. "My brain just isn't wired that way, to be able to see something beautiful and artistic made out of something that is neither. Ella Garcia has the same ability you do."

"Everybody's good at something different. Most people can't do what you do."

"But they could if they tried. If you gave me ten pieces of scrap metal, you know what I'd do with them?"

"Take them to the dump?"

"Recycling, and probably cut myself and get tetanus in the process."

By the time they'd finished eating all the pizza they wanted and she'd convinced him to take the leftovers home with him, Devon had relaxed from her initial nervousness. Cole was oddly easy to talk to. She knew plenty of guys, and would consider several friends, but none would fall into the category of close friends, not like her and Mandy. She wondered if maybe their charade would lead to a true friendship between her and Cole. Despite being attracted to him, she found she liked the idea.

She instinctively started to pull her wallet from her purse.

"Put that back," Cole said. "We're supposed to be on a date, remember?"

"Plenty of people go Dutch on dates."

"You think that will convince your mom we're a couple?"

"Oh fine, go and make a good point."

The smile that spread across Cole's face made her insides do a little zingy thing that wasn't wise if she wanted to keep on the path to friendship and nothing more.

Cole tossed enough money on the table for the bill and tip. "Come on, little lady. Let's blow this joint."

She snorted at his affected drawl.

"Nice," he said, teasing her about her reaction.

"What do you expect when you sound like a really bad character from an old movie?"

"Now, that's no way to talk if you want a second date."

Before she could respond, Cole draped his arm around her shoulders and pointed them toward the exit. It was all Devon could do not to melt from the blast of desire that hit her. Not good, not good at all.

Cole leaned close to her ear. "I'm doing all the work here."

With her heart pounding, she wrapped her arm around his waist. Oh heavens, he felt as good as he looked and smelled. The man was solid muscle. At least it felt that way. A fast-motion parade of what she'd like to do with him raced through her head.

"You okay?" he asked.

Get it together, Devon, before he figures out you're having a difficult time acting as if his touch isn't affecting you.

"Yeah. Just ate too much."

"You ate two pieces of pizza."

"They're big pieces." Which was true, but less of a reason for why she limited herself than her determination not to return to the overweight teen she'd hidden under her voluminous clothes.

On their way out, they met Elissa and Pete Kayne. Elissa wasn't able to hide her surprise at seeing them together, and Devon fought the urge to step away from Cole and admit her subterfuge. But then the thought of her mother crowing that she'd been right and forcing an introduction to yet another man in whom Devon had no interest had her gripping Cole a little tighter.

"Well, this is new," Elissa said. "My aunt is losing her touch as unofficial town matchmaker if people are managing to get together all on their own."

The look Elissa gave Devon promised more questions whenever the guys weren't around.

Devon really hadn't thought about how their lie would grow out in all directions like a spiderweb. She just hoped she didn't get stuck in it with no way to pull herself back to safety.

After a bit of chitchat, Pete held the door open for Elissa. Cole, his arm still draped casually around Devon's shoulders, escorted her to her car. She had the craziest thought that he might kiss her goodbye, but he most likely wasn't willing to go that far with their charade.

When they reached her car, Cole removed his arm from her shoulders. She missed the warm weight, the bit of intimacy she liked more than she should. As she dug for her keys in the bottom of her purse, Cole crossed his arms and leaned back against her car.

"Think we got enough people talking that your mom will buy it?"

"It's Blue Falls. Chances are pretty good. I'm surprised my phone isn't ringing already."

"At least you don't have to face your mom's eager questions when you get home."

"Your mom wants us to get together for real?"

"I think she'd be overjoyed. That's why you need to be the one to reaffirm with her that we're just friends. Hopefully she'll listen to you."

Though Devon didn't think it would take much for her to get on board with Barbara's thoughts, it was nice to hear Cole refer to them as friends. Totally separate from her attraction, she liked being around him and wouldn't mind being able to hang out even after their trickery was over.

Or could they just keep on pretending forever?

She shook her head at that thought, knowing her friends and neighbors and parents too well. If she and Cole went too long without taking things to the next level, without a ring appearing on her finger, people would wonder and ask questions, ones she wouldn't be able to answer without coming clean or telling more lies.

"Don't worry. I'll hold up my end of the bargain."

"Okay, good night, then." He pushed away from the car.

"Good night."

She wanted to watch him walk toward his truck, drink in the sight without him noticing, but that wasn't conducive to reminding herself that they weren't a real couple. She slipped into her car and headed toward home. For the first time in she-couldn't-remember-how-long, she wasn't looking forward to the quiet that would greet her when she got there.

Chapter Five

When Devon arrived at work the next morning, she dreaded walking in the door. She'd venture a guess that there was a fifty-fifty shot her mother would be waiting for her again. But it wasn't her mom who met her when she stepped inside A Good Yarn. It was Cole's.

"Good morning, Barbara," she said, glancing at Mandy, who was refilling some of the soap bins. "What can we do for you?"

"I had to come to town for some groceries and thought I'd stop in to see how your date went last night."

Devon rounded the counter and stowed her purse away. "You didn't ask Cole?"

"I did. Guys aren't much for details."

"Not much to say. We ate pizza, talked about high school some. We went home."

Barbara sighed, causing Devon to remember her promise to Cole.

"You know we're just pretending, right?"

"So you don't like Cole?"

"I like him fine. He's a nice guy."

"That's not what I mean."

Devon momentarily tripped over her own tongue as she tried to force out another lie. Those things had a way of multiplying.

"We're just friends."

The gleam in Barbara's eyes told Devon the older woman had noticed how Devon had faltered in her answer. Allowing his mom to hope wasn't what Devon had promised to deliver for him.

"Barbara, I know Cole has told you this, but he's not interested in a serious relationship. And I can't blame him. He's been burned twice. Can't say I'd be thinking any differently in his shoes."

"People say those types of things until they find the right person."

"Well, if that happens, then you both can be pleasantly surprised."

"Fine, I'll stop pushing."

"Thank you."

"Moving on to a different topic, I'd like to ask you a favor."

"Okay," Devon said, admittedly with some hesitance.

"I'd like a different set of eyes to help me figure out how to set up my quilts for the Arts and Crafts Trail. Cole might have a lot of talents, but staging and decorating are not among them."

Devon wasn't convinced this wasn't just another tactic to get her and Cole together, but how could she say no? She liked Barbara, and they both wanted the trail to be a success for everyone involved.

"Sure. How about tomorrow afternoon?"

"Perfect. I'll bake cookies so we can have some snacks while we ponder."

Devon barely had time to take a breath after Barbara left before Mandy was standing across from her, staring at her expectantly.

"What?"

"Okay, really, how did the nondate date go? I want more details than you gave her."

"Honestly, we ate some pizza, talked and then we left."

"Now, see, I ran into Elissa this morning, and she tells a different story."

Devon sank onto her stool, wondering just how big this snowball was going to get as it raced down the mountain. And if it was going to run right over her and bury her alive.

"He put his arm around my shoulders as we left, just a little extra visual for the gossips to take back to Mom."

"Uh-huh," Mandy said, not sounding convinced that Devon was telling the whole story. Well, she wasn't, was she? "And did you touch him back?"

"What are we, fourteen?"

"This is way more fun than anything we talked about at fourteen. Though, come to think of it, there might have been some hormonal pining away for Cole Davis back then, as well."

"I'm not pining away for Cole."

"Did you pawn your libido or something?"

"Mandy Richardson, why are you pushing this?"

The teasing fell away as Mandy braced her hands against the counter. "Because I heard something in your voice when you were defending Cole to your mom."

"I don't like how she looks down on good, hardworking people. You know that."

"I get that, and it's admirable. But it was more than that. You forget how long we've been friends, how well I know you. And I can tell there's more going on than just a bit of drama to fool your mom."

"Okay, fine, I find him attractive," Devon said, not

sure if she should be relieved that she could admit the truth to someone. "But it's under control."

"Why?"

Devon pointed toward the front door. "You heard what I said to Barbara. Cole isn't the least bit interested in a romantic relationship."

"But you wish he was."

"Would I be opposed? No. But if I want my mother to respect my wishes, I've got to respect his."

"You're playing with fire here."

"I'll be fine."

Thankfully a couple of women, tourists judging by the fact that Devon had never seen them before, came into the store, saving her from further interrogation. But it didn't prevent her mind from racing, imagining what it would be like to date Cole for real. To have him hold her in his arms, kiss her, make her forget all about the pressure her mother constantly put on her.

Dang it. One fake date and already she was losing the battle to think of Cole as a friend and nothing more.

COLE LIFTED THE welding helmet and wiped the sweat from his face with a towel. After a morning of checking on the herd and installing a new water trough, it was nice to be in the shade of the barn despite the fact that he was still hot. He examined the seam where he'd welded two pieces of rusty scrap metal together to form the back of the horse's leg. Not too bad, if he did say so himself. Loads better than the mess he'd made on his first several attempts at sculpting six months ago. Maybe the anger had gotten in his way then. Lord knew he'd had enough of that banked inside him.

He looked toward the entrance of the barn when he heard footsteps. When he saw Devon, he wondered if she was here to request a second fake date already. Not that he hadn't enjoyed himself as they'd eaten pizza. He had. She was more talkative than he remembered. And there wasn't the pressure of expectation when he was with her. Sure, they might have different views on finding "the one," but he didn't begrudge her wanting that. At one time, he'd wanted it, too.

He stepped through the open stall door. Devon caught sight of him and yelped as she stopped so quickly she nearly tripped. Her eyes widened in surprise.

"Sorry to startle you," he said.

She looked away, beyond him, and waved off his concern. "I was looking for your mom but didn't get an answer at the house."

"She's gone to deliver a quilt. She ought to be back soon."

"I guess I should have called ahead."

"Something I can help you with?"

She still didn't make eye contact, and he wondered if she'd endured another unpleasant run-in with her mother. Though he was sure Devon was perfectly capable of taking care of herself, he had the oddest urge to protect her. Not that he should be surprised. After all, his dad had instilled chivalry and a protective instinct in him and Cooper from the time they'd been able to walk and talk. Despite his less-than-successful love life, that ingrained instinct remained.

"No, I'll just wait for your mom. She wanted some design help setting up her space for the Arts and Crafts Trail. Though honestly I think it's a thinly veiled ploy to get the two of us in the same general area."

"And you went along with it?"

At that she finally met his gaze. "Hey, I tried setting her straight, but I don't think she believed me."

"Maybe you weren't persuasive enough."

She looked startled at his words, and he realized it might have sounded like an accusation.

"That didn't come out right, sorry. I'm just saying when my mom gets an idea in her head, it's hard to dislodge. I'm normally all for her determination, but this is one thing she needs to let go."

"I'll try again."

"Thanks. In the meantime, why don't you come in for something to drink? I could use something, too."

"I don't want to impose."

He actually laughed at that. "Accepting a soda is far from imposing. Not like requiring dates."

Devon's mouth fell open, making him laugh again.

"You could have said no," she said.

"I could have. What can I say? I'm a good guy."

"And modest, too."

He smiled at her sarcasm as he grabbed his shirt where he'd hung it on a hook and pulled it on over his tank undershirt. "Come on. I feel like I could drink the town water tank dry."

Devon fell into step beside him. He shortened his strides to match hers.

"Heard from your mom?"

She shook her head. "No, and I don't know whether to be thankful or worried."

"That's what you wanted, her to back off."

"Yeah, but I know my mom well enough to know that it won't last long. She really likes getting her way."

They stepped inside the house. "I don't get it. Is her goal of picking your husband more important than you being happy?"

"She honestly believes that she knows what's best

for me, that if I would just go along with her choice, then I'll be happy."

"Sounds like your mom has some control issues."

"Ya think?"

Cole crossed to the fridge and asked, "What kind of drink would you like?"

"Water is fine."

"You sure? We've got Cokes, lemonade—"

"I actually prefer water."

"Okay."

She'd had a Coke with dinner the night before, but maybe she made exceptions for pizza. Water with pizza was just wrong on so many levels. It required Coke or a cold beer.

As he placed their drinks on the table, he noticed the storage container his mom used for cookies in the middle.

"Looks like Mom made cookies."

"She told me yesterday she was going to."

"Yep, she's trying to get you to switch to her side, all right."

"I can't be bought with cookies."

"You're a rare woman indeed."

Devon punched him lightly on the shoulder before she took a seat at the table.

Cole popped the lid off the cookie container and found his mom's delectable chocolate-chip cookies, the kind that when you ate them, you could literally taste the butter.

"You've got to have one of these."

"I'm not hungry. Still full from lunch."

"You don't have to be hungry to eat my mom's cookies. There's a separate corner of your stomach reserved for them."

She laughed, and it hit him again that Devon was pretty, with a little more force this time. Well, of course he was aware she wasn't ugly by any stretch, but the laughter and the smile that accompanied her pretty features made it obvious that she was attractive in that natural, effortless way.

She accepted the cookie he offered her and bit into it. And proceeded to close her eyes and savor that flavor he knew so well.

"I think I just gained ten pounds with that one bite," she said.

"Mom's cookies are worth every pound, too."

He watched her hesitate before taking another bite. Cole devoured the rest of his cookie then grabbed another.

"I know your mom gives you a hard time," he said. "What about your dad?"

"He's too busy with work to notice what I'm doing. He doesn't push like Mom does, but he doesn't stop her, either."

Cole glanced at the cookies then around the homey kitchen that had been part of his entire life. In this room, his mother had cooked for her family. They'd all sat around this table eating, joking and laughing, and discussing decisions about the ranch countless times. If he had to venture a guess, there hadn't been many warm-and-fuzzy family dinners in the Newberry house. Devon hadn't even had a sibling with whom to commiserate.

"I'm sorry you didn't have the type of childhood I had."

"It could have been worse. I mean, I never had to worry if I'd be able to eat or if I'd have a roof over my head. I had friends who did."

"Still, money can't buy happiness."

Devon placed the uneaten half of her cookie on her napkin. "Not many people believe that, at least in my experience. And it's hard to feel sorry for the kid who can have whatever she wants."

"I'd guess there were things you wanted that you still haven't gotten." Like unconditional love and support, the kind of priceless things his parents had given him and Cooper despite some lean years during droughts or illness in their cattle herd.

Her gaze caught his and it felt as if she was examining his mind to see if he meant what he'd said.

"You're perceptive. Nobody but Mandy has ever gotten that. At least not that I know of."

"Is that why you do all the homemade and sustainable stuff, to differentiate yourself from your parents?"

"Some, yes. Initially that was probably the impetus, but it all spoke to me like nothing else ever has. It just feels right. I enjoy it."

"I understand that, going after the thing that is just who you are. You hang on to it."

"I'm really sorry you had to give up rodeo."

The sympathy in her voice didn't bother him like the well-meaning words of so many others had. While he hadn't doubted the sincerity of most people when they'd said it, there hadn't been depth to their words. But Devon, it felt as if hers came from the deepest part of her. Maybe she'd imagined her shop and farm being ripped away, leaving her floundering and wondering what to do with the rest of her life.

"Thanks."

"Do you still like to go to rodeos, or is it too difficult?"

"I haven't been to one since I've been home. Been too busy."

That was only partly true, despite the fact that he had been busy making repairs and updates to things his mom hadn't been able to handle on her own since his dad's passing. She'd had part-time help with the herd, but other things had gone by the wayside. But if he were being honest, he'd admit that he didn't know how he'd react if he was around all those familiar sights, sounds and smells again but as an outsider, no more than a spectator.

"We should go to the one this weekend. The proceeds are going toward Christmas presents and a Christmas carnival for kids and their families who might not have Christmas otherwise."

"Well, I guess I'd be a jerk if I said no to that." He supposed he couldn't avoid going to rodeos for the rest of his life. Might as well pull the bandage off the wound and be done with it.

The front door opened, making him realize he'd been so involved with his conversation with Devon that he hadn't even heard his mom's car pull up outside.

"Sorry I'm late, dear," his mom said as she hustled into the kitchen and patted Devon on the shoulder. "I took a quilt over to Martina Rutherford, a gift for her daughter's wedding shower, and we got to talking and time flew by. Oh, you should see Shailene's wedding dress. She's going to look like a princess on her big day."

Talk of weddings—that was his cue to leave. He stood, drawing his mom's attention.

"I didn't mean to run you off."

"You're not. Got some fencing to replace out on the west side of the pasture."

"Well, thanks for keeping Devon company while I

was gone. That was nice of you." The little gleam in his mom's eyes had him refusing to comment. Instead he headed toward the great outdoors, where he'd be free of anything remotely resembling walking down the aisle toward inevitable failure.

"YOU TWO LOOKED like you were having a nice time," Barbara said the moment the door closed behind Cole.

"He just offered me a drink and one of your amazing cookies while I waited for you." She'd already told Barbara there was nothing romantic between herself and Cole, so either the older woman would believe it or not. Despite what she'd told Cole, Devon didn't think repeating herself was going to change Barbara's opinion. It might instead seem as if Devon was protesting too much.

"Glad to know I raised the boy right." Barbara motioned for Devon to follow her. "Well, we better get to it. I appreciate you coming out."

"No problem. Happy to help." Even if she was still recovering from the sight she'd seen in the barn. When Cole had stepped out of that stall wearing jeans and a white tank-style undershirt, his skin shiny with sweat and a few streaks of dirt, she'd darn near swallowed her tongue. If she'd managed to hide her reaction from him, it was no small miracle.

Her first thought after the fact that the man was so damn sexy she'd been in danger of her very bones melting was that she'd made a huge mistake in delving into their fake romance. How could she pretend with him when her body screamed for it to be real? Even now as she followed his mom out toward a small garden shed, Devon couldn't stop replaying over and over that moment he'd stepped into her line of vision.

"What do you think?"

Devon jerked her attention back to Barbara and realized she'd missed whatever the other woman had said. "I'm sorry."

When Barbara gave her a knowing grin, Devon realized she had to talk her way out of this, for her own sake and Cole's.

"I've been distracted by some things my mom said the last time I saw her."

"Maybe letting your mom get to you just perpetuates the cycle," Barbara said. "I know she's your mom and you probably love her, but your mother is a bully and a snob. Always has been. And the only way to win with people like that is to not feed the beast. Instead of arguing with her, pretend like what she says doesn't bother you. It will drive her up the wall."

"That is much easier said than done." But the memory of how Mandy had responded to her mother popped into her head. Devon had very nearly seen steam come out of her mother's ears when Mandy had replied to Devon's mom in that flip "I don't care what you think anymore" way. Maybe her best friend had been living and breathing the answer right in front of Devon and she hadn't noticed it.

"Most things are, sweetie, good and bad."

While Devon helped Barbara decide on a pale shade of yellow to paint the interior of the shed, suggested she plant flowers along the front and gave her opinion on how best to display the quilts, part of her mind was fixed on determining how to deal with her mother. If a new tactic worked better than how she'd been reacting up to now, then she could call off the fake relationship with Cole. She was surprised by how much she hated that idea, but that told her it was probably the best plan.

Again, thinking it and actually going through with it were two different things. The truth was she liked spending time with Cole, even if she'd have to work harder not to let her very real attraction show.

Chapter Six

Devon spent the final few minutes of the store being open on Saturday brainstorming ideas for her anniversary celebration. Her task served a dual purpose—she needed to nail down the details and it kept her from being nervous about that night's "date" with Cole at the rodeo.

Okay, so the latter half of that wasn't working so well. It hadn't helped when she'd seen him drive through town earlier in the day, pulling a cattle trailer behind his truck. Seriously, how could a guy look so good just driving a pickup?

She'd considered calling him and canceling, but she hadn't been able to force herself to do it. She knew that with each minute she spent with him it was going to be that much more difficult to end their arrangement, but she evidently was a glutton for emotional punishment.

She refocused on the list of ideas she had written down but glanced up when the door opened. Cole stepped through looking every delectable inch the rodeo cowboy. A Western-style, button-up shirt covered what she knew were some truly fabulous arms and chest. That seemed a shame, but then she found she didn't want every woman in Blue Falls ogling him, either.

Sure, that was a tad possessive, unwisely so, but the truth was the truth.

"I thought we were meeting at the fairgrounds," she said, amazing herself at how normal and unaffected she sounded. Too bad she hadn't gone into acting. She'd be a shoo-in for major awards.

Cole leaned his forearms against the front counter across from her and glanced around the store before fixing his gaze back on her. "If we were really dating, we wouldn't always be driving separately."

This was it, the perfect opportunity to tell him he didn't have to pretend to date her anymore. He had enough on his plate running his family's ranch and working on his art without having to make time for her. But then the image of her mother with a satisfied smile popped into her head. Followed quickly by the depressing thought of not having an excuse to spend time with Cole anymore. Would they go back to just exchanging a quick hello when they happened to bump into each other in town? After even the little time she'd spent with him recently, the idea of losing their budding friendship hurt.

"I guess you're right," she said. "What's next? Bouquets delivered to my door?" She laughed a little, trying to play off how the idea of him sending her flowers for real made her heart speed up.

"You never know," he said with a teasing smile. "Something huge and expensive. Wouldn't that surprise your mom?"

"Sure would." Not to mention Devon. Cole didn't seem like the type of guy to spend a shameful amount of hard-earned money on something that would wither and die in a few days.

Cole pushed away from the counter and stood to his full, impressive height. "You about done here?"

"Yeah." She grabbed her purse and shoved her notepad inside, then hopped off the stool, her turquoise cowgirl boots clunking on the polished wood floor. She smoothed her brown and turquoise broomstick skirt and rounded the counter.

"You look nice."

She almost heard her boots skid as she stopped suddenly. "Uh, thanks."

"Don't sound so surprised."

What did that mean?

Don't read too much into it.

She waved in his general direction. "You don't clean up bad yourself."

"I guess anything would be an improvement over the last time you saw me."

She wouldn't say that, but she made a vague sound of agreement and moved toward the door. Cole opened it and allowed her to precede him before stepping out onto the sidewalk himself and waiting as she locked up.

Devon turned away from the door just in time to see Verona Charles watching them with a huge smile on her face. Uh-oh. As if they didn't have enough attempted matchmaking going on with Barbara, now the town Cupid had spied them together. But since they were supposedly already together, maybe she'd move on to someone else.

"Well, don't you two look picture-perfect," Verona said. "I've got to admit, I hadn't thought about pairing you two up, but it couldn't be a better match." She shifted her gaze up to Cole. "Don't you agree?"

"Yes, ma'am, I do." Cole's hand captured Devon's, his fingers sliding between hers with an ease that would have made more sense if they were actually a couple and held hands often.

Devon's blood electrified and raced through her at a speed that she feared wasn't healthy.

"I know your mother must be so happy," Verona said to Cole.

Devon noticed how Verona said nothing about her mom.

"As a clam. It was nice to see you, Verona. We've got to head out. Don't want to miss any of the rodeo action."

"You two have fun. And tell your mom hello for me."

"Will do." Cole tugged lightly on Devon's hand, pulling her out of her stunned state enough that she was able to walk next to him toward his truck.

She knew he probably kept his fingers entwined with hers because Verona was watching, but for those few moments, she allowed herself to pretend that he was holding her hand because he wanted to, because being near her made his heart thump as wildly as being near him did hers.

When they reached his pickup, he continued to hold her hand until he'd helped her up into her seat.

"Thanks," she said.

His gaze met hers, level because of how high up she sat.

"You're welcome." Cole hesitated for a moment before stepping back and closing her door.

As he walked around the front of the truck toward his side, Devon finally drew in a deep breath. Yep, she'd traded one problem for another. She'd had a lifetime of dealing with her mother's expectations. But the crazy, runaway feelings she was having toward Cole? Those were new territory, and she realized she might have made the biggest mistake of her life asking him to pretend to be her boyfriend.

Needing desperately to focus on anything other than how Cole's strong, work-roughened hand had felt wrapped around hers, Devon pulled her notepad out of her purse and started perusing her list of celebration ideas.

"What do you have there?" Cole asked as he slipped into his seat and started the truck's engine.

Devon tried not to be disheartened that he seemed totally unaffected by their brief hand-holding. And why would he be affected? Their faux relationship was nothing more than a mutually beneficial favor to him. Remembering he'd asked a question, she held up the notebook.

"Ideas for my shop's anniversary celebration."

Cole pulled out onto Main Street and headed for the fairgrounds. "Let's hear 'em."

Latching on to the safe topic of conversation, she recited her grocery list of ideas.

"The kids' knitting class should be popular," she said.

"Why not include adults, too?"

"I guess I could."

"I bet my mom would do a quilting class or demonstration if you asked her to," Cole said with a glance toward Devon.

"I don't want to take away from her work. I know she stays busy."

"Are you kidding? She'd love it, combining quilting with chatting everyone up. Plus, it would give her some extra exposure for the launch of the Arts and Crafts Trail."

"Maybe I'll ask her."

"She'll probably have a boatload more ideas for you, too."

The drive to the fairgrounds was over almost as soon as it began, and Devon's nerves started firing again. Would Cole reclaim her hand, or had that simply been for Verona's benefit so she'd spread the news far and wide?

As soon as Cole parked, Devon shoved her notebook into her purse and hopped out of the truck. Cole met her at the front.

"You're stealing my chances to be the doting boy-friend," he said as he pointed back toward the passenger door.

"Sorry. Habit." She started toward the entrance gate, and Cole walked close to her but didn't take her hand or drape his arm around her shoulders. While she missed the contact, she had to remember they were only friends and she could expect Cole's acting to go only so far.

When Cole paid their way in, she added her half to the mental tally she needed to repay him. Guys might insist on paying during real dates, but that wasn't what this was, any of it.

Though he still didn't touch her, Devon sensed Cole's hand near the lower part of her back as he accompanied her through the crowd toward the grandstand. She perused the bleachers, looking for an empty spot. Enthusiastic waving drew her attention to Mandy, who was sitting next to India Parrish and Keri Teague, along with several other members of the Teague family.

"Mandy, right?" Cole said next to her.

"Yeah."

"I think she wants us to sit with her."

Devon smiled. "How could you tell?"

"Wild guess."

A jolt of awareness went through Devon's body as Cole gently touched her elbow. It was nothing more than a chivalrous gesture, supporting her as they climbed the steps to the higher row, but it jangled her already frazzled nerves anyway.

"Hey, you two," Mandy said, all bright and chipper as if she'd just won the lottery, learned chocolate wasn't fattening and landed Prince Charming at the same time. The look she gave Devon fairly screamed, *I'm up to something!*

When they took their seats, Mandy leaned forward to speak to Cole past Devon. "You probably don't remember me from high school—"

"Sure, I do. You two were always together," Cole said as he glanced at Devon.

He remembered that? Devon could almost believe he hadn't been aware of her existence, except for that pivotal moment when he'd defended her against Amy.

"I'm surprised you remember," Mandy said, echoing Devon's thoughts.

"Wasn't that big of a school."

And way to burst the bubble of potential happiness, dude.

More chitchat passed back and forth between Mandy and Cole, then Cole and Ryan Teague behind them. Devon, feeling strangely left out, a feeling she really hated, focused her attention on the grand entry beginning in the arena.

As soon as the entry and the national anthem were over, she noticed how Cole's attention firmly fixed on the riding and roping events. He sat on the edge of his seat, even giving instruction under his breath. But when the final event, the bull riding, was about to begin, she sensed a change in him. Though she wasn't touching him, she could tell his body stiffened. He watched the animals in the chutes as if sizing them up, judging their moods and personalities. She supposed it's what he'd done for years when he'd been among the cowboys about to risk his life astride one of those huge beasts.

She wasn't sure how she was able to read him so easily, but she could tell he hated being in the stands right now. He wanted to be down there in the midst of the action, about to test his skill in the arena. He'd said he hadn't been to a rodeo since returning to Blue Falls, and she knew in that moment it wasn't just because he was busy on the ranch. Even as busy as ranch life was, he could have spared two or three hours to watch a rodeo. But being able to only watch a sport he loved as a career, that he'd been good at, was hard for him.

Before she could think better of what she was doing, she slipped her hand into his, fingers entwining, palm to palm.

Cole shifted his attention from the rider who'd just been tossed into the dirt to her. There in his eyes, she saw a longing that she understood all too well.

COLE KNEW HE missed life on the rodeo circuit. He'd even expected twinges at tonight's rodeo, the first he'd attended since retiring. But he hadn't been prepared for the intensity of the longing. It'd been manageable, about what he expected, at first, but it had built as the night went along. By the time he saw the first of the bull riders preparing to ride, it felt as if his insides were being squeezed. Bull riding had been his life for so long, since he'd graduated high school, that it still didn't feel real or final that he'd never do it again.

The feel of Devon's hand clasping his startled him. At first he thought that she'd seen someone, perhaps her mother, who needed convincing of their supposed romantic relationship. But when he turned his head and saw her expression, the truth of her compassion stole his breath. One look told him that she knew what he was feeling and sympathized. It wasn't pity, but rather a heartfelt wish that she could return what he'd lost. The purity of her silent offer of support touched him so deeply he didn't know how to react. How could this woman who until recently had been only a past acquaintance understand perfectly when his own mother and brother, even his riding buddies, didn't fully understand? Sure, none of them had gone through it, but neither had Devon.

He smiled and squeezed her hand, not wanting to let go of that connection. Maybe that was dangerous considering his vow not to get attached to another woman, but at the moment he didn't care.

"Thanks."

She simply nodded and went back to watching the riding.

Though he watched as well, almost perfectly predicting what the riders' scores would be, a lot of his attention remained focused on the feel of Devon's small hand in his. He had the strangest sensation that it was easy, simple, without expectation. Giving rather than taking. That was a switch from his two marriages.

No, he couldn't think like that. He and Devon were friends. He was doing her a favor.

But you were mighty quick to say yes to playing her boyfriend.

Unwilling to let his brain go down that road, he refocused his attention on the next rider up. Based on what he knew, this would be the toughest bull of the night.

"Next up, we've got Adrian Wells riding Cotton-Pickin' Good," the announcer said.

The bull, a monster in size, showed his displeasure by rattling the gates. A sick feeling curled in Cole's stomach, and two seconds after the gate opened he knew why. Wells was jerked to and fro as if he were as flimsy as a piece of rope. And then he went airborne. In the blink of an eye, he slammed into the ground and lay still.

Beside Cole, Devon gasped and gripped his hand with a sudden strength that surprised him. He placed his other hand atop their clasped ones.

The bull fighters rushed in to protect Wells as the pickup guys steered Cotton-Pickin' Good out of the arena. Other cowboys jumped down off the gates where they were sitting, and Cole knew things weren't good when one of them whistled for the paramedics.

"Oh, my God," Devon said. "Is he—?"

"Knocked out." At least he hoped that's all it was.

The entire grandstand of people watched, hushed, as a paramedic hurried into the arena while another backed up the ambulance. When the driver hopped out, the paramedic kneeling beside Wells, who still hadn't moved, called something back to the driver. Cole couldn't make it out, but it became obvious what he said as the driver pulled a backboard out of the ambulance.

Though Cole had seen a similar scenario countless times before, had even been the one hauled out on more than one occasion, it didn't stop the sickness in the pit of his stomach. It eased only marginally when he saw Wells move one of his legs. Thank God, not paralyzed. But Cole knew from experience that he could have serious injuries, perhaps ones that would end his career.

When Wells was finally on the backboard and lifted

by half a dozen fellow cowboys, everyone in the grandstand stood and clapped for him. He was aware enough to lift his hand in a quick wave.

Instead of continuing to watch Wells be carried out, Cole looked at Devon. "You ready to go?"

The quickness with which she nodded told him the scene had upset her. Without thinking, he took her hand in his and headed toward the steps as she said goodbye to Mandy and the others. Cole just wanted to be anywhere other than where he was at the moment.

When they reached his truck, he hesitated letting go of Devon's hand. Surely he wasn't allowing his feelings to change toward her. They had an arrangement, nothing more. The need for connection now was simply a reaction to being in a situation that brought back memories he'd rather not relive. Holding her hand gave him something else on which to focus.

"You've been through something like that before, haven't you?" she asked.

He reluctantly broke contact with her and leaned against the front of his truck, staring toward the arena where the ambulance was pulling away and the rodeo staff was preparing for the final couple of riders of the night.

"Yeah, I've had my share of scares." He nodded at the arena. "That was eerily familiar."

"The reason you retired?"

"Yeah. We've all had broken bones, torn muscles, more cuts and bruises than you can count. But the last time I rode, I got thrown, hit hard and it further damaged some vertebrae in my back. The doctor who saw me said I was done, and the way he said it made me believe him."

"I'm glad you quit."

He shifted his gaze to Devon.

"Nothing is worth damaging yourself beyond repair," she said. "You had a good, successful run. And now you're starting a second career, something that you're also really good at."

The belief in her voice stirred something within his chest, something that made him determined that they'd remain friends after their charade was over.

"I appreciate it."

"It's not just flattery," she said.

"I know. You don't seem the type to offer false praise. I mean, you're kind but honest."

"Except when lying about our relationship."

For a crazy moment, he thought about saying that maybe they didn't have to be lying about that. And then he remembered how easily he'd been led down that path twice before and how he didn't want to go through that again.

He shrugged. "There are way worse lies. I'm not even sure this counts."

She laughed a little. "Somehow I think my mom would beg to differ."

"She never has to know. Whenever you're ready to call it quits, we'll stay friends. We won't give her a big, public breakup scene to pounce on."

She met his gaze and studied him for a minute.

"What?" he asked.

"Thank you."

"You've already thanked me."

"I know, but in all honesty, you barely know me. Doing this for a virtual stranger is no small thing."

"It's not as big a deal as you seem to think. It isn't like it's hard to spend time with you."

Quite the opposite, in fact.

"Thanks, I think."

He smiled when he glanced over to where she was leaning against the truck beside him. "Are you fishing for a better compliment?"

"Who, me? Never."

He bumped his shoulder against hers. "Let's get out of here."

How many times had he said that to a woman and meant something totally different? As he glanced at Devon as she turned away, he wondered why she wasn't dating someone for real. Surely some man with a brain and who hadn't been handpicked by her mother had crossed her path. A man who hadn't sworn off serious relationships, he reminded himself when he remembered how her hand had felt in his. How in that moment when their gazes had connected and he'd seen her understanding, it would have been so easy to lean over and capture her mouth with his.

Way too easy.

And a really, really bad idea.

Chapter Seven

Cole likely had no idea how his words had made Devon's mind go wild with images that were never going to be more than just fantasies in her head. As he drove back toward downtown, she kept reminding herself that his "let's get out of here" did not have the same meaning attached to it that those words normally did when a guy uttered them. Not that she'd had loads of experience being on the receiving end of that meaningful phrase.

He'd just wanted to leave the rodeo, and she couldn't blame him. After what she'd witnessed, she wasn't so hot on staying, either. Her stomach was still twisted up inside her at the idea of how easily that bull rider could have come down wrong and broken his neck, been gored or even killed. And how many times Cole had risked his life riding. She fully understood following one's dream, but at least her dream never put her life in danger.

When Cole parked behind her car, all her racing thoughts distilled down into one. She had to end their charade before it got out of hand.

"Hope you had a good time tonight despite how it ended," Cole said when he turned off the truck's engine.

"I did, thanks." She hesitated for a moment.

"You sure about that?"

She glanced over at him and was struck anew by

just how handsome he was. Now that she knew him a bit better, had seen his kindness and his humor, he was even more attractive. Which was not a good thing for her peace of mind.

"Yeah." She took a quick breath then dived into what had to be said. "Listen, I wanted to thank you for being willing to do the whole fake-dating thing, but the more I think about it the more I realize how unfair it is. I pulled you into a lie that I shouldn't have."

"Seems I remember volunteering."

"People offer all kinds of things to be nice, never expecting the other person to take them up on it."

"So you think it was an empty gesture?"

"No, that's not what I mean."

"Devon, just stop. You're worrying for no reason. I like hanging out with you. I've been away for so long that the friends I had in high school have such different lives than I do now. I mean, we're still friends but not close. They've got jobs, wives, kids and all that comes with those things. It's nice to have someone to just have fun with."

How was she supposed to respond to that? She couldn't very well say no because she was afraid spending more time with him would only make her like him more.

"Okay, if you're sure."

"Trust me when I say there are way worse things than pretending to date a pretty woman."

An extra jolt hit her heart. Had he just called her pretty? Even if he wasn't thinking romantic thoughts toward her, that simple comment filled her with a joy that wasn't wise but that there was no stopping.

"Well, I better get home," she said as she reached for the door handle.

"Wait," he said. He hopped out of the truck and hurried over to her side to open the door.

"This isn't necessary," she said when she allowed him to hold her hand as she slipped out of the truck. "No one is around."

He glanced beyond her for a moment then started to lower his head toward her.

Oh, my God! He was going to kiss her. Her heart thumped hard, like it was trying to break through the ribs imprisoning it.

But in the next moment, he whispered close to her ear, "Your parents just walked out of La Cantina."

"Oh," she managed, perhaps a bit too breathy.

Whom was she kidding? She sounded like she was about to cry out with release. At least in her mind she did.

She tried to calm her pulse and her breathing, but she lost control of both when he planted a soft kiss on her cheek. It took all her waning willpower to not turn so that her lips met his.

Several torturously long seconds passed before Cole took a step back. She made the mistake of meeting his gaze. Was there any hope her feelings weren't visible, hanging there between them doing their best to scare him away?

"Uh, they're driving away," he said.

"Okay."

A couple more seconds ticked by in slow motion before Cole seemed to remember he was standing too close to her and took a couple of steps back, releasing her upper arms. He broke eye contact and motioned toward her car.

"I'll wait until you're safely inside."

Though Blue Falls was about as safe a place as she

could imagine, it still touched her that he wanted to ensure her safety before heading for home himself.

Devon hoped the shakiness she felt in her legs didn't show as she walked toward her car. When she reached the driver's side door and opened it, she glanced back at Cole.

"Good night, Cole."

"Good night, Devon."

As she sank into her car, she couldn't help imagining Cole whispering good-night to her as they drifted off to sleep beside each other.

The entire drive home, she replayed the feel of his hands on her arms and that beautifully terrifying moment when she'd thought he might kiss her. She called herself a fool for thinking that only moments after he'd been talking about how she was definitely in the friend zone. If he was the kind of friend who'd pretend to date her, who would plant a warm kiss on her cheek in an effort to keep her mother at bay, how was she going to survive that friendship?

When she walked through her front door, Honeysuckle greeted her by entwining herself around Devon's legs. Devon leaned over to pick up the buff tabby. Honeysuckle proceeded to nuzzle Devon's cheek very near where Cole had kissed her.

Cole had kissed her!

Okay, so it was on the cheek and just another part of their romantic ruse, but it was still so much more than she could have even imagined only days ago.

"I suppose you're hungry," she said and placed the cat back on the floor.

Just as she finished filling Honeysuckle's bowl, her phone rang. Her heart started that banging-to-break-free thing again as she wondered if Cole might be calling her. But when she saw it was Mandy, she tried not to be disappointed.

But she hid that disappointment when she answered the call. "Hey."

"Hey, yourself. You okay? You and Cole left kind of quickly. I was sort of hoping it was so he could ravish you."

"Ravish? Really? Who even uses that word anymore?"

"It's a perfectly good word for a perfectly good time."

Devon rolled her eyes. "When the rider got hurt, we just didn't feel like watching anymore."

"I heard he's going to be okay. Sore, but okay."

"That's good." A tremendous amount of relief allowed the tension camping out within her to lessen. Even though she didn't know the man, she was thankful he hadn't been seriously injured or worse. Again the image of Cole lying motionless in the dirt threatened to make her sick.

"You're falling for him, aren't you?"

"What?"

"Cole. I saw how you took his hand, how you two looked at each other."

"You are imagining things. We're pretending in order to stem my mother's assaults, remember?"

"Maybe at first."

"What's that supposed to mean? We've been out exactly twice. We're friends, that's it."

"You don't have to pretend for me. I know you better than that."

Devon walked to her living room and sank into her favorite chair. "I tried to end our little act tonight, but Cole didn't want to."

"Oh, really?"

"No, it's not like that." She told Mandy what he'd said about it being nice having a single friend with whom to hang out.

"Friends? Are you sure he's not just using that as an excuse?"

"Trust me. He has about as much interest in a serious relationship as I do in walking down the aisle with the next guy my mom plops in my path."

But he'd lingered a little after that kiss, hadn't he?

No, she was imagining it, or it had simply been for her parents' benefit.

"Well, that's disappointing," Mandy said. "Though I'm still not one hundred percent convinced."

"I can't think that way."

"Because you like him?"

"Yeah. I'd have to be brainless and blind not to. But that doesn't change anything, and he's right. It is fun hanging out together. Surely time will erase any non-friend feelings and it'll all be okay."

When Mandy didn't respond, Devon feared she knew what her friend was thinking.

"You think this is all a mistake, don't you?"

"I just worry that you're going to end up getting hurt."

Devon had to admit, at least to herself, that she was beginning to fear the same thing.

She was still worrying about it after hanging up with Mandy, when she received a call from her mother. Of course receiving a sweet kiss from Cole without her mother having something to say about it was too good to be true.

"How did your date go?" Cole's mom asked as soon as he walked into the house.

"Fine, as far as fake dates go."

"I thought you'd be out later."

"We both have to work in the morning. Ranches and stores don't run themselves." He almost told her about the rider who'd been injured, but he stopped himself in time. He might be home now, but Cooper was still out there riding. His mom didn't need another vivid reminder of the danger her youngest son put himself in each time he climbed onto the back of a bull. "Speaking of, Devon might be calling you about doing some sort of quilting class at her shop."

"Oh, that might be interesting."

"She's doing a special event for the anniversary of her opening."

"Maybe you should do something, too."

He laughed as he kicked off his boots next to the front door. "I doubt she wants a welding iron in the middle of her shop."

His mom sighed. "You might have a point there."

Cole wandered into the kitchen when his stomach growled, reminding him he'd not eaten anything for dinner. A pang of guilt hit him. Even if it had been a fake date, he should have offered to get Devon something to eat.

He grabbed a cold, fried chicken leg and stepped to the sink to eat over it.

"You didn't have dinner?" his mom asked as she joined him in the kitchen.

"Nope." He'd been too busy paying attention to the rodeo, talking with people he hadn't seen in a while. And then there'd been that moment when Devon had captured his hand with hers, giving him support he hadn't even realized he needed.

He sensed his mom wanted to say something else, but she refrained. Instead, she walked across the room and into the laundry room. He wondered if she was brainstorming another way to get him on the topic of Devon. Wanting to avoid that, perhaps for a different reason than he'd had only the night before, he ate the rest of the chicken leg and washed his hands.

"I'm beat. I'll see you in the morning."

"Okay."

Had she just given up a little too easily? Deciding not to risk finding out, he beat a retreat to his bedroom. But after chucking his clothes, he sank onto the edge of his bed and realized that he might not be going to sleep anytime soon. His brain kept coming back to that warm, comforting feeling that had spread through him when Devon had taken his hand. He couldn't shake the feeling that the moment had been special, important, one that somehow created a bond between them that no amount of joking around and pretend dating ever could.

He thought about her driving home alone and found he wanted to make sure she'd gotten there safely. But that would seem odd when she'd made the drive countless times before. Still, he picked up his phone and started a text to her. He stared at the empty text box for a few seconds before figuring out a way to check on her without saying he was checking on her.

Told Mom about the quilting class idea. She says it sounds interesting.

After hitting the send button, he stared at the phone for several long seconds. No response came, and he tossed his phone onto his nightstand, reminding himself that they were friends, that he didn't want anything more than that. He was mistaking his reaction to her kindness for something more.

He slid into bed and turned out his light, but damn if he didn't just end up staring at the shadows on the ceiling. When his phone buzzed with a text, he chose not to think too hard about how quickly he grabbed the phone to read it.

Okay. Thanks.

Her response seemed abrupt, not like the person he'd begun to get to know over the past few days.

Everything okay?

Again, she didn't respond immediately.

Yeah, fine.

He'd swear he could hear the tone of her voice in the two-word text, and it said that all was not fine.

Your mom?

He watched the screen, telling himself that he was just concerned for a friend. He wasn't going to focus on the odd thought that he wished he was with Devon to comfort her as she had him earlier.

Let's just say she's not a fan of PDA, says it's crass.

Because of the kiss?

Again, a hesitation.

Yeah.

Sorry.

Maybe he'd taken the pretending a little too far, but he'd not given it that much thought. He'd gone with his instinct. Warning bells should be going off that his instinct had been to plant a kiss on her cheek, but they weren't. Maybe that should be the biggest warning bell of all.

Another text from her appeared on his phone.

Don't worry about it. I'm used to it.

He'd swear he could hear the resignation in her voice, and it made him angry that her mother was so hard on her. Devon didn't deserve it. After getting to know her again, really for the first time, he didn't understand how anyone, especially her mother, could be so harsh toward her. Everything he'd seen and heard pointed toward Devon being a good, kind person, which was a miracle considering her mother's personality. It made him like Devon even more, and he wanted to find a way to cheer her up.

Resorting to teasing, he typed a response. So I guess she would have had steam coming out her ears if I'd really laid one on you, huh?

A rush of heat ran through him at the image that brought to mind. It was dumb to allow himself to think of Devon that way when he didn't plan to act on it. Or maybe it was better to just let his brain wander where it wanted to since he was safely miles away from her, where he couldn't make an even bigger mistake and do something that might lead her to think there was a future for them.

If she would even want such a thing.

The memories of all their interactions zipped past like a recording on fast forward. A look here, a smile there, the tenderness when she'd taken his hand. Was she interested in making their relationship a real one? Or was he inserting meaning where there wasn't any? History had shown he wasn't the best at reading women.

He wondered if he'd gone too far with that last text, if maybe Devon couldn't tell he was teasing.

Or was he? Was he fishing to see how she'd respond?

Forget steam. More like flames.

He chuckled at her response. That sounds painful.

It does, doesn't it?

He imagined her smiling, hoped he'd made her smile.

I'm not keeping you awake, am I?

No. I was pacing when you texted. Probably cursing a little.

You, curse? I'm shocked!

Ha. Ha.

They continued texting back and forth, everything from more jokes about how they could rile her mother to her plans for her anniversary celebration to tales from his rodeo days.

He typed a new message. Hope you have unlimited texting.

I do. But I should probably hit the hay. I'll be dead on my feet tomorrow.

Sorry to keep you up so late.

Don't apologize. I enjoyed it. I feel better now.

I'm glad.

Good night, Cole.

Good night, Devon. He damn near told her to have sweet dreams but caught himself in time. That was more than a friend would say. That stepped over into real romantic relationship territory.

When he slipped his phone onto his nightstand, he stared up at the ceiling and wondered if Devon was doing the same. He was certain he'd never texted that much with anyone in his life. Anytime he was dating anyone—hell, even married to anyone—he'd actually talked on the phone or in person. So why did he feel like the texting back and forth with Devon was more intimate?

Here in the safety of his own room, he allowed himself to wonder what things might have been like had he gotten involved with Devon first, or even second. Anytime before his two divorces had soured him on long-term relationships. She was so different from both Amy and Bridget. He couldn't help but think that maybe he'd been a bigger idiot in high school than he'd previously thought. Had he stuck with Amy despite signs he shouldn't and overlooked someone who might have been a better match?

He shook his head on his pillow. There was no rewriting the past, and he doubted he and Devon would have worked out any better than he and Amy, though it likely would have been for a different reason. Considering she still put up with her mother's meddling so she could stay in Blue Falls, there was no way she would have accompanied him on the road. He couldn't imagine her waiting at home for long stretches while he rode the circuit either.

No, Devon had made a good life for herself doing the things she wanted despite the way her mother tried to steer her daughter's life. She believed in finding her very own Prince Charming, and he couldn't be further from that description.

He needed to stick to the plan, simply helping out a friend with a bit of harmless fibbing. Remembering that he'd made a promise to himself of never making the mistake of a "lifelong" commitment to a woman again.

Chapter Eight

Cole pulled out of the feed store's parking lot and pointed his truck toward home. But when he reached the downtown area, his gaze landed on A Good Yarn. If he and Devon were really dating, people would expect him to stop to see her if he was in town, right? Maybe take her out to lunch as a surprise.

He knew full well that he was walking awfully close to the line between fake and real but he told himself he wouldn't take the step over. It wasn't as if he was going to walk into her store and take her up against the nearest display counter.

Cole's hands gripped the steering wheel tightly, and his heart rate shot into overdrive at that image. He whipped into a parallel parking space but didn't immediately turn off the truck's engine. Instead, he wondered if he should have agreed with Devon when she'd said they should stop pretending.

What the hell was wrong with him? Couldn't he just be friends with a woman?

Yes, he could, and he was going to prove it to himself even if to everyone else it would appear that he and Devon were a couple.

He turned off the engine and jerked the keys out of the ignition. By the time he reached the front door to A

Good Yarn, he'd told himself about a dozen times that he was just imagining any attraction toward Devon. It was only because he hadn't gone out with anyone for real in a long time, and he was still stinging from Bridget's betrayal.

He and Devon were friends, and on the road to being darn good ones based on how easily they'd texted for nearly an hour the night before.

When he opened the door and stepped inside, it wasn't Devon he saw inside but rather Mandy. She smiled, a little too mischievously for his liking, and lifted a ball of purple yarn.

"Looking for something to do in your spare time?"

He huffed out a single laugh. "I wouldn't know the first thing to do with that except maybe play with a cat."

She tossed the yarn into a wooden bin with dozens more of its multicolored cousins. "Devon isn't in this morning."

"She okay?"

Mandy tilted her head a bit. "You sound concerned."

Too concerned? Why did it matter?

"I know she had another run-in with her mom last night."

Mandy looked surprised. "That was after she went home."

"We texted a bit."

"Did you?" Mandy crossed her arms and gave him a look that said she thought there were some juicy details she didn't know yet but planned to find out.

"Yeah." He wasn't going to give her anything else, especially when he was still in the process of convincing himself that sticking with his "no relationships" policy was a good idea.

"Why are you doing this?" Mandy asked.

"What?"

"Pretending to date Devon?"

"You know why."

Mandy lifted an eyebrow. "Do I?"

He shook his head. "What is with this town? It's like you've all been infected with a matchmaking virus."

"So you're not interested in Devon?"

"As a friend." He braced his hands against his hips. "I don't like people who bully their children, even if they're not little kids anymore."

He must have finally convinced her because she sighed and seemed to deflate a little as he watched.

"Just tell Devon I stopped by, okay?" he said and turned toward the door.

"You may talk to her before I do. I doubt she's going to come in today. If I know Devon, she's venting her frustrations by burying herself in work."

Cole grabbed the doorknob and opened the door.

"I'm sure she wouldn't mind some help," Mandy said.

He pretended he didn't hear her as he left, but damn if her parting words didn't plant themselves in his head. Once again, he started toward home, but at the edge of town he pulled a U-turn and headed toward Devon's farm.

He might be a fool, but it wouldn't be the first time.

WHILE DEVON LOVED her shop, it felt good to stay at the farm and not have to face anyone today. It seemed her mother was becoming more persistent in her efforts to run Devon's life, not less. If not for her text conversation with Cole the night before, Devon would really be in a funk this morning.

She smiled as she milked one of the goats. Though she knew she shouldn't have allowed it to go on as long as it had, the texting back and forth had been nice. More than nice. And it had been easier in a way than talking to him face-to-face. Since he couldn't see her, she didn't have to hide her expressions or the way she nearly held her breath while waiting for his next response. She'd hated ending the conversation, but she really had been tired. Not to mention she felt as if she were close to falling for him, and that would be the least wise thing she'd ever done.

Still, it had been nice, had come right when she needed it. For that she was thankful.

She finished the last of the milking and picked up the two buckets and headed toward the house. Halfway there, she heard someone pulling into her driveway and looked up.

No. It couldn't be.

And yet it was. She watched as Cole parked and stepped out of his truck. Devon barely resisted the urge to drop the buckets and retreat back into her barn. What was he doing here? And why did he have to show up when she looked dreadful?

She tried to tell herself it didn't matter, that it shouldn't because they were just friends, but it did matter. Well, there was nothing she could do about it now, stuck halfway up the hill from the barn to the house.

Cole hurried down the hill toward her. "Let me take those."

"I've got them." She almost took a step back, but Cole captured the bucket handles. To keep from losing the milk, she let go. "What are you doing here?"

"Saw Mandy and she said you were playing hermit today. I came to see if you needed a hermit buddy."

"A hermit buddy? Doesn't that negate the whole hermit thing?"

"Details, details."

Despite the fact that she had to look a fright and that being near Cole caused her nerves to vibrate, she smiled at his response.

Cole lifted the buckets as if they weighed no more than glasses of milk. "Where do you want these?"

Devon led him toward the house, trying to remember if it was in a big mess. She wasn't a slob, but she didn't have much company other than Mandy, either. Once inside the kitchen, she directed him to set the buckets on the countertop.

"So this is what you make your soap out of?"

"It's one of the main ingredients, yeah." She opened a drawer and pulled out the freezer bags and set about scooping fresh milk into the bags to freeze for later use.

"You hold the bag and I'll scoop," Cole said.

She stopped and turned toward him. "Really, why are you here?"

"I'm avoiding cutting hay."

Devon didn't believe him, at least not entirely. She communicated that by crossing her arms and raising an eyebrow.

He shrugged and leaned back against the kitchen counter. "Not sure. Just felt like maybe you could use the company."

"I stayed home to be away from people for a day. I didn't want to inflict my foul mood on anyone else."

"So I failed in my attempt at cheering you up."

"No, it's not that. I appreciate you getting my mind off things, but it's my mom, you know? It's not like she's going away." Devon braced her hands against the edge of the sink. "I love my mom. I just wished she'd at least try to see things from my perspective and respect that I'm an adult entitled to make my own decisions."

"Has anyone tried to talk to her on your behalf?"

"Mandy tried, but let's just say that Mom has never particularly liked Mandy despite the fact that the two of us have been best friends since we were kids."

"Maybe I—"

Devon shook her head and met Cole's gaze. "No offense, but Mom wouldn't listen to you, either."

"Because I'm not good enough for her, for you."

A thrill raced through Devon's body at the idea that he might want to be good enough for her, though she knew he was talking about her mother's point of view.

Before she could think, she placed her hand atop his. "You're more than good enough. My mom just wouldn't approve of anyone she didn't suggest."

Her heart shuddered at the way he looked down at her, how his lips parted. Did she imagine him leaning ever so slightly her direction?

In a move of self-preservation before she convinced herself of things that weren't there, she lifted her hand from his and grabbed one of the freezer bags.

Cole, thankfully, moved wordlessly to scoop the milk into the bags as she held them open. They worked in silence for several minutes. Devon tried to ignore how much easier the task was with Cole helping. She had to figure out how to halt her growing feelings for him without killing their friendship. If she shoved him completely out of her life, he'd figure out why. And she didn't want him to know how she felt if he didn't reciprocate. Even if he might feel some smidgen of attraction, that's all it would ever be. She'd heard with her own ears the absolute certainty that he would never have a serious relationship again.

"I don't like how your mom treats you. You don't deserve it."

"You barely know me."

"I know you're a good person, and you deserve to be happy. Your mom is making you the exact opposite."

"Cole, it's not that bad. I've got a good life. My farm, my business." She smiled up at him. "Good friends."

"Just with one big thorn in your side."

"If that's the worst thing I ever have to deal with, then I'll count myself lucky." But she couldn't help but wonder what life might be like if her mother stopped trying to make her decisions for her. If Cole liked her as more than a friend.

Well, neither of those things was going to happen, so she might as well stop allowing them to take up space in her mind and heart.

"Are you avoiding your own mom by being here?" she asked.

"Not today. She might have finally accepted she's fighting a losing battle."

"Oh." Devon grabbed a few of the bags of milk and carried them to the deep freeze in the pantry. "Well, I guess that means you're not getting anything out of our arrangement anymore. That doesn't seem fair."

She turned to find he'd followed her and stood a little too close for her comfort. He lifted his hands to her shoulders, causing her breath to halt in its tracks.

"Forget the deal, okay? From now on, we're just friends hanging out. Let everyone think what they like."

"But you kissed me." Oh, no, had she said that out loud? "I mean, I know it was because my parents were nearby."

"And I'm sorry that it caused more harm than good."

"No," she said, shaking her head. "It's fine. If it hadn't been that, it would have been something else."

She looked up at him in time to see his jaw tighten,

and her heart thumped extra hard at the way he seemed to want to come to her defense.

In the next moment, he removed his hands from her shoulders and took a step back. "What do you say we just do some work and forget all about matchmaking mamas?"

"Sounds like an excellent plan to me." She knew she should encourage him to leave and see to his own work, but the truth was she didn't want him to. Tomorrow she'd figure out a way to extricate herself from this mess of her making without letting Cole know why, but today... Today she was going to enjoy being with him and try to teach her mind how to think of him as a good friend and nothing more.

BY THE TIME afternoon started fading into evening, Cole thought he had a pretty good handle on how to make goat's-milk soap, more than a passing idea of how wool from sheep ended up as those colorful balls of yarn in Devon's shop, and a growing amazement at all the things she could and did do to make her life her own.

When she'd invited him to stay for dinner, he insisted she let him cook.

"You're my guest," she said. "That wouldn't be right."

"You've been on your feet all day."

"So have you."

He grabbed her by the shoulders and turned her toward the living room. "Stop being so stubborn."

"You're hijacking my kitchen?"

"Yes, and you're going to like it."

"You sound mighty sure of yourself."

He guided her to a chair and urged her to sit.

"You know we became friends because someone was

trying to tell me what to do," she said as he walked toward the kitchen.

He stopped and turned halfway back toward her. "You're not supposed to be thinking about your mom."

She stared back at him and something about her expression changed, something he couldn't quite name.

"You're right."

As he worked on making baked mac and cheese, they talked back and forth about what she'd settled on for her anniversary celebration.

"I'd like to display one of your sculptures outside the shop if you have something that would work," she said.

He stopped midmotion and looked toward the doorway to the living room. Though he couldn't even see her, she'd somehow touched him again. His mom believed in his work, but she was his mom. She had to. But from the moment Devon had seen his sculptures, she'd told him how much she liked them, how much talent she thought he had. He hadn't realized how much he needed someone else to believe he could do something besides ride bulls and keep the ranch from falling into the red, some external validation to combat the doubt he had every time he put flame to metal.

"Cole?"

"I'll see what I have."

A few minutes later, he had everything on the table and walked into the living room. He stopped beside Devon's chair and extended his arm.

"Your meal is ready, madam."

She stared at him for a moment like he'd lost his mind. Maybe he had, but if so then losing his mind felt pretty good.

Devon shook her head and smiled. "I think maybe

you fell off one too many bulls and addled yourself permanently."

She wrapped her hand around his proffered arm, and he escorted her into the kitchen like...well, like they were on a real date. He didn't mind that idea as much as he should.

Damn, he shouldn't be here. Devon was a forever kind of woman, but he couldn't give her that.

"Something wrong?"

He realized he'd stopped walking. *Quick, idiot, think of something.* He extended his hand toward the table. "The offerings of Chef Cole."

She took a couple of steps toward the table, then looked back at him. "Did Mandy tell you I like mac and cheese?"

He shook his head. "No, it's just something I can actually make. It's the one good thing that came out of my second marriage, my ex-mother-in-law's recipe."

"Well, it's my favorite food, so bonus friend points go to you."

They made their way to the table and filled their plates with the mac and cheese as well as steamed broccoli and some olives he found in the fridge. He watched as Devon took her first bite of the main dish.

Devon's eyes closed and she moaned in a way that had a sudden and unexpected effect on the part of him that was thankfully hidden from her view.

"That's it, you've ousted Mandy from the best friend slot."

He laughed at that. "You'd regret that. I'd be terrible at chatting about whatever you gals talk about, clothes and makeup and stuff."

Devon snorted. "Yeah, because I'm obviously such an icon of fashion."

"You always look nice."

She glanced down at her clothes then met his gaze. "Yep, I'm ready for the catwalk."

"I see nothing wrong with how you look."

"Then you're blind."

"You look like a woman who has been doing something she loves all day."

"Riding in a tornado?"

He tossed a broccoli floret at her. "Cut it out."

"Hey, don't waste food."

As they ate, their conversation flowed so easily from one topic to another that it surprised him. Though it shouldn't since it had been easy to talk to Devon since that night he and his mom had rescued her from Angela's clutches.

"Can I ask you a personal question?" she asked as they sat with empty plates and full stomachs.

"Yeah."

"What happened with your second wife?"

How many times had he wished he could just erase his second marriage? Amy, at least, he could chalk up to youthful ignorance. With Bridget, well, he'd just been an idiot. He considered changing the subject, but it felt like maybe it was time to lance that particular wound to stem the festering.

"I got hurt."

Devon leaned her forearms on the table. "I don't understand."

He thumped the edge of his plate as he tried to figure out where to start. The beginning, he supposed.

"I met Bridget at a rodeo a couple of years after Amy and I got divorced. She's the cousin of one of the ropers. I'd thought I was good with just playing the field, but the next thing you know, I was popping the question. I thought everything was fine until I got hurt and missed a trip to the National Finals. Turns out she was tired of waiting for me to make the big time and she saw my getting hurt as a further delay of her being able to be the wife of a world champion and everything that goes with that."

"She cared more about your bank account than your health and well-being?"

The shock in Devon's voice made him smile despite the bad memories.

"Seems I have a knack for falling for women who care more about what I can give them than me. I wasn't able to give either of them what they wanted, and so they left." Two big blows to his ego, not to mention his heart.

"Well, they're both stupid. I'm sorry that you got hurt, but you're better off without them."

He smiled at the passion behind her words. "You're right, though I gotta say it felt like a kick to the gut both times."

"Honestly, there are women out there who make me weep for my gender. They're more interested in status and things than in having a loving, honest relationship."

He suspected she wasn't just talking about his exes anymore, but he didn't mind. The fact that she was so angry on his behalf did funny things to his insides. Devon Newberry might have come from a privileged background, but that wasn't what made her worth a thousand of Amy or Bridget. She was kind, genuine, hardworking, funny—all the things he liked in a woman.

Nope, he couldn't be thinking about her that way. But his brain and other parts of his body weren't getting the message.

It would pass. It had to. He really did like having

Devon as a friend, and he wasn't willing to jeopardize that.

"Well, there are good women in the world, too," he said, realizing he'd let several seconds tick by. "My mom and you come to mind."

"I'm honored to be in the same company as your mom."

It seemed everything that came out of Devon's mouth made him like her even more. And thinking about her mouth led to other thoughts...

He slid his chair back and stood. When he reached for the dirty dishes, Devon grabbed his wrist.

"No, I'll clean up."

"I don't mind."

"I do. You cooked, so I'll clean. House rule."

He looked at her offer as the opportunity he needed to leave before he made a mistake he couldn't take back.

"Okay. I need to get going anyway."

"Yeah, your mom probably thinks you got lost."

Devon walked him to the door, and he had to force himself not to think about kissing her good-night. He told himself it was just because he hadn't been with a woman in months, nothing more. But when she smiled at him, he was afraid it was more than that.

Oh, hell.

Chapter Nine

Devon rearranged the display of candles again, decided she didn't like it and put it back the way it was. Something just wasn't right.

"You know you've changed those at least a dozen times today, every time you walk past them," Mandy said.

"Something about the way they look is bugging me."

"That's not what's bugging you."

Devon looked at her best friend. "What do you mean?"

"You haven't talked to Cole in a couple of days, and you've gotten more fidgety by the hour."

"That's not true."

"Who knows you better than anyone?"

Devon opened her mouth to say…something, but the words didn't form. Instead, she simply said, "You."

"Bingo."

Devon sighed. "I don't want to feel this way about him because I know it can't go anywhere."

"Are you sure about that? I mean, he spent the entire day at your house the other day, kissed you just to help convince your mom that you and he are a genuine thing."

"It wasn't a real kiss."

"And the all-day–hang-out session?"

Devon walked past Mandy toward the front counter. "Just friends hanging out. Believe me, there's nothing there."

"Fine," Mandy said as she followed. "Then you need to find someone who will be the real thing."

"Please tell me you're not going to set me up, too."

"Nope, but I think you should try online dating. It'll expand your pool of possibilities outside Blue Falls, and maybe you'll find that Mr. Right who'll make you forget about Cole Davis."

Devon couldn't imagine that happening, though it would certainly alleviate a lot of the twisted-up feelings that had taken up residence in her middle. The day at home with Cole had been great, beginning to end. But now she wondered how wise it had been to allow him to stay considering Mandy was right. With each hour that went by with not a peep from Cole, her heart hurt a little more.

Seemed Cole wasn't the only one who fell for the wrong person.

Deciding that she didn't want to be the type of woman who pined away for an unrequited love, she pulled the laptop in front of her and started comparing dating sites.

"You're really going to do it?" Mandy asked, obviously surprised.

"It was your suggestion."

"And I thought it would take a lot more arm-twisting."

"I feel like taking a big step outside of my comfort zone before I think about it too much and talk myself out of it."

"Who are you, and what have you done with my best friend?"

Devon stuck her tongue out at Mandy. "Don't you have work to do?"

"Nope, all caught up. You're paying me to stand around and bug you mercilessly."

"Good to know. Well, make yourself useful and help me set up a profile so I don't sound like a desperate old maid."

They spent the next several minutes checking out the various sites before she settled on one. Next came creating a profile that was appealing but also honest.

Mandy was in the midst of taking several pictures of Devon for the profile when the front door opened and Cole walked in. Why did he always have to look so good that it made Devon's heart feel as if a colony of butterflies had invaded her chest? Why did he have to be a confirmed bachelor?

"Oh, perfect timing," Mandy said and stepped up beside him, phone in hand. "Which of these photos of Devon do you think is most appealing to guys?"

"Mandy," Devon said, trying to hide her horror at what her best friend was doing.

"What?" Mandy tried to look all innocent, but Devon knew her well enough to see the well-meaning deviousness in her friend's eyes. "You make an online dating profile, you need a picture that will draw guys' attention. Cole is a guy. We need his perspective."

Devon wanted to go hide in the stockroom until Cole left. Then she might actually pack up and leave Blue Falls from the embarrassment.

"Online dating?" Cole said, sounding surprised.

Devon had to remind herself that she was not hearing any sort of resistance to the idea of her move toward online dating. But the way he looked at her, even for just a moment, made her wonder.

But then he took the phone and started scrolling through the photos. "I guess this means I'm getting dumped."

He laughed a little, but it seemed as if it was a bit forced.

No, that was her hopeful imagination again, which told her that she was making the right move. Sure, she'd have to live with her mother's "I told you so" about Cole not being right for her for the rest of her life, but that had to be better than losing her heart to a man who wouldn't be giving his to her.

Deciding to joke right back, she said, "It's been fun, but a girl's got to have some variety."

Mandy barked out a laugh, and Cole responded with only a lifted eyebrow before going back to looking at the photos on Mandy's phone.

Devon tried not to fidget as Cole seemed to consider each photo carefully. Was he thinking they were all terrible? That she was making a mistake? She couldn't help but wish that he might not want her to sign up for online dating because he wanted to be with her, but he'd said nothing of the sort, done nothing that would give her hope beyond what was probably just her imagination.

When he suddenly stepped forward toward the counter, Devon startled so much she almost fell off her stool.

"You okay?" Cole asked when her gaze met his.

"Uh, yeah. Foot slipped."

He smiled the slightest bit, and for a moment, she thought that maybe he could tell she was lying and why.

Cole extended the phone to her rather than Mandy. "This one. Shows your personality best."

"I'm not sure that guys who go onto dating profiles are overly concerned with personality."

"Then you don't want to date them."

Devon's breath caught for a minute as her mind searched for an appropriate response. "Physical attraction is important to a relationship. It shouldn't be everything, of course, but it can't be discounted."

Thus her intense attraction to Cole, which was only strengthened as she got to know him and the type of man he'd become.

"I'm going to go grab some lunch from the Primrose," Mandy said. "Anyone want anything?"

Devon shifted her attention to Mandy, silently screaming, "What are you doing? You got me in this mess, now get me out!"

"I'm good," Cole said.

"Not hungry," Devon managed while silently promising to get Mandy back later.

Mandy grabbed her purse, shot Devon a smile Cole couldn't see, and headed out the door.

Once she was gone, Cole leaned his forearms on the counter. "So, was this your idea or Mandy's?"

"Little of both."

"Your mom still giving you trouble?"

She shook her head. "No more than normal. It's just...well, I'm not getting any younger. I really appreciate how you've helped me out, but I'm ready to find someone for real."

If only the man she'd already found felt the same way.

"Take your time, and be careful. I don't want to see you get hurt."

He couldn't know how much his words touched her heart, how much she'd love to place her palm against his cheek and tell him how he'd come to mean a great deal to her. Instead, she smiled a little and said, "Thanks."

"I brought you the sculpture you requested."

The abrupt change in subject caught her off guard, and it took a moment for her brain to switch gears. "Oh. Great."

He nodded toward the door. "Come on."

She followed him out onto the sidewalk and gasped when she saw the six-foot-tall metal sculpture made to look like a bouquet of flowers. Her thoughts went back to the day they'd gone to the rodeo, how she'd teasingly asked him if bouquets delivered to her door were going to be part of the fake-dating scenario. Had he remembered that? And if so, could this beautiful metal bouquet mean anything other than she'd asked for a sculpture and he'd happened to have this one on hand?

"It's beautiful." She ran her fingertips along one of the petals. "I don't remember seeing it before."

"Probably because I made it last night."

Her attention shot to him. "You made this in one night?"

He shrugged. "Couldn't sleep."

She turned her attention back to the sculpture, noting all the amazing detail considering it was basically made of old junk.

"You like it?"

"I love it. I'll be sad when it sells. I mean, happy for you, of course, but sad to see it go."

"It's not for sale."

Her heart skipped a beat as she turned her gaze back to Cole. "But you have to make money on your sculptures."

"I will, hopefully, but this one is a gift."

She shook her head. "I don't understand."

"Can't a guy give a friend a gift?"

"Sure, but this is too much."

"If it makes you feel better, having it sitting here in front of your shop might draw some business for me."

She thought about it for a moment, finally accepting the amazing gift because it could be great publicity for his fledgling artistic endeavors.

"Thank you. It's…" She swallowed against sudden tears she simply couldn't show him. "It's the most wonderful gift anyone has ever given me."

"Good. Now I don't feel so bad asking for a favor."

She laughed. "Oh, so not so much a gift as payment, huh?"

"No, it's yours no matter if you grant the favor or not."

Devon turned toward him and crossed her arms. "Okay, out with it."

"I need a partner for the Canoe Fest on Saturday."

"You signed up without a partner?"

"Correction, my mom signed the two of us up. I just found out about it over breakfast this morning."

Devon knew that if she was going to begin distancing her heart from this man, she should say no. The idea of riding around the lake with him in a canoe was a bad idea, even if it was to raise money for a good cause, helping people struggling to pay medical bills while promoting exercise as a health benefit.

She must have hesitated too long in responding because Cole said, "Come on, what do you say to one last fake date before you find Mr. Right?"

"Sure." She forced the single word out before the lump rising in her throat could prevent it. "The anniversary celebration will be over by then, so it'll be nice to have a day away from the shop."

And one last outing with Cole before she nixed their pretend romance.

SEVERAL TIMES ON the way home, Cole found himself gripping his steering wheel much harder than necessary. It shouldn't matter to him that Devon was looking to start the dating game for real, but it did. He tried telling himself that it was because, as he'd claimed, he was concerned about the kind of men she'd meet, that they'd treat her well. But a voice that refused to be silenced kept telling him to stop lying to himself. He liked Devon, more than he should. If he'd known his traitorous feelings would head in this direction, he never would have offered to help her out with her mom, at least not by pretending to date her.

When he reached the ranch, he pulled through one of the gates into the pasture and headed toward a small cluster of trees. He pulled up and shoved the truck into Park and got out to deposit a salt lick for the cattle on the ground.

The task occupied his thoughts only for the short time it took to complete. As he slid into the driver's seat again to head for the next drop point, those thoughts went right back to Devon and the situation he'd gotten himself into.

He was already second-guessing the wisdom of letting his mom convince him to honor the commitment she'd made on his and Devon's behalf for the Canoe Fest. Sure, he liked the idea of canoeing around the lake with Devon. They always had a good time when they were together. But if his feelings were changing, best to just make a clean break, especially if she was looking for that happily-ever-after he no longer believed in. He didn't want her thinking that by his hanging out with her too much there was more between them than friendship. He couldn't allow there to be. Twice burned and all that.

When he exited the pasture an hour later and drove toward the house, his thoughts veered away from Devon when he saw the familiar pickup truck sitting next to his mom's car.

As soon as he parked, his younger brother came sauntering out of the barn with their mom.

"Well, look what the cat dragged in," Cole said as he pulled Cooper into a quick shoulder bump and slap on the back.

"Had to come see if what Mom has been telling me is true. Big bro done gone and became a sculptor." Cooper grinned like he found the whole thing funny, just the type of reaction Cole had honestly feared from anyone who knew him. It was a big leap, and an unexpected one, from bull rider to artist. Devon's glowing praise had made him forget that concern.

"One word and I'll dunk you in a stock tank."

"You'll try," Cooper said with a grin that made him popular with the ladies and always proved a pain in the butt for Cole.

"Come on, you two," their mom said as she hooked one of her arms around Cole's and the other around Cooper's and led them toward the house. "I don't get to have both of my boys home at the same time often, so you're going to behave and make this old lady happy."

They both gave her a grudging "Yes, ma'am" as they had when they were kids. But as they entered the house and the three of them went about pouring glasses of lemonade and sitting at the kitchen table, Cole relaxed some. It was nice to see his brother, even if he didn't say it. Though he'd admit to himself that it stung a bit, as well, knowing that Cooper was still living the life that Cole had had to leave behind.

"So, Mom tells me you're dating Devon Newberry. Didn't see that one coming," Cooper said.

Cole slowly turned his head toward his mom and

gave her the stink eye. "Did she also happen to mention that Devon and I are just friends, that we're putting on a show so her pushy mother will leave her alone?"

"Pretend dating? Yeah, right."

Cole shifted his attention back to Cooper. "Yeah, right."

Cooper lifted his hands, palms out. "Okay. Don't be so touchy."

Cole knew he was likely revealing too much of his changing feelings toward Devon, so he needed to change the topic.

"What about you? Who's the latest woman on Cooper Davis's arm?"

"In between at the moment. Got to focus on riding."

That pang hit square in Cole's gut again, but he acted as if it didn't bother him. Seemed he was getting good at pretending lately.

For the rest of the day, Cole and Cooper caught up on each other's lives as they worked together around the ranch repairing a water pump and doctoring a few head of cattle that had contracted pink eye before it spread. Despite how much he missed riding bulls himself, Cole was glad to hear Cooper was doing so well. Of course he knew that since he kept track of his brother's results, but it was good to hear it from the man himself.

After dinner, Cole left his brother joking with their mom in the kitchen and made his way out to the barn. He hadn't intended to work on a sculpture, but he found himself picking up a piece of metal and determining where and how to add it to the horse work in progress.

"You know I was just giving you a hard time earlier, right?" Cooper said as he ambled down the center aisle of the barn.

"About what? There's so much to choose from."

Cooper pointed toward the sculpture. "It's damn good."

Cole snorted, waiting for the inevitable punch line.

Cooper propped his arms along the outside of the stall where Cole was working. "I couldn't picture it when Mom told me, but I'm impressed."

"You're not feeding me a line right now?"

"Nope, for once I'm dead serious."

Cole looked back at the piece he'd put countless hours into. "Thanks."

"Doesn't mean I'm not going to tease the fire out of you about Devon."

His brother just couldn't help himself.

"Believe what you want, but my view on relationships hasn't changed."

"I didn't say you had to marry her. Though thinking of you as a member of the Newberry family is weird in an alternate reality kind of way."

"Well, you don't have to worry about that."

"I can't blame you, though Mom seems to think there's more between you and Devon than you claim."

"That's because Mom wants grandkids and believes in the fairy tale like she had with Dad." Only even that fairy tale hadn't had a happy ending. All those happily-ever-after stories never mentioned that eventually the happy couple would die, most likely one before the other, leaving the other half alone.

Damn, those thoughts went dark.

"You know you can date without putting a ring on her finger, right?"

"We're just friends, man. And besides, Devon is looking for Prince Charming. We all know that's not me."

"Well, that's true."

Cole wished he had something to throw at Cooper.

Instead, he called him an unflattering name that just made his brother laugh.

Cole set his mind back on work, trying not to focus on the fact that Cooper was watching. It meant more than he would have expected to have his brother offer him a genuine compliment on his work, giving him more confidence that he'd made the right decision to try his hand at art. He might have had to leave bull riding behind and would never give up ranching, but the metalworking fed something inside him he'd never known existed.

"So, since you're not interested in Devon, maybe I'll swing by and visit her, see if she's as pretty as Mom says."

Cole ground his teeth to keep from telling Cooper to stay the hell away from Devon. That would give credence to the feelings he was trying to deny.

"She won't be interested."

"Because she's already interested in someone else?"

"Because she wants forever with someone, and you'll be scooting out of town in a few days at most. How long are you staying, by the way?"

"Trying to change the topic?"

"Just stating facts."

"Whatever you say."

What the heck was going on? Why did it seem the entire universe was pushing him and Devon together? Well, except for her mother.

Maybe it was a good thing she was doing the online dating thing, before he went and did something stupid like starting something he couldn't finish.

Chapter Ten

As Devon looked over her store full of kids and their parents, a combined sense of excitement and nervousness washed over her. Though she'd been hyping her store's anniversary celebration, she hadn't expected such a great turnout for the children's knitting class. Several of the moms and even one dad were also taking part in the beginner lesson.

She stopped next to Mia Monroe to check her progress on her knitted bracelet. "That looks good. I like that shade of purple."

Mia looked up at her with a huge smile. "Thanks."

Devon smiled back, then moved on to check the next child's work. The front door opening drew her attention, and she couldn't help the leap of her pulse when she saw Cole stepping inside behind his mom. He carried a pile of folded quilts in his arms, ones she assumed Barbara was going to use as part of her demonstration after the knitting class was over.

"I'll be right back," Devon said to the knitters, then crossed to the front of the store. "Can I take something?"

Barbara shook her head. "Just show me where you want me. I've got plenty of arms to help me today."

As if to give evidence of her claim, Cooper Davis

stepped into the shop carrying a plastic tote and gave Devon a huge grin.

"Mom was right. You are beautiful."

Devon's mouth fell open a bit at the unexpected compliment. Her gaze shot immediately to Cole, who looked like he wanted to wring his brother's neck. Why was that?

Before she could begin to answer that, a couple of women stepped inside and past Cooper.

"Can I help you?" Devon asked.

"Yes, I was wondering about the sculpture you have out front. I didn't see a price on it."

Again, Devon's gaze shot to Cole for a moment. He looked surprised that anyone had even noticed the gorgeous piece, let alone asked about it.

"That piece isn't for sale, but you're in luck. This is the artist." She indicated Cole, who seemed a little startled before he extended his hand to the women.

The woman who'd asked about the sculpture smiled in a way that Devon recognized and didn't particularly like. But she had no right to feel that way, and if Cole was true to what he'd claimed since they'd become friends, it didn't matter.

"Nice to meet you," he said.

Devon forced her attention to Barbara. "Let's get your area set up."

As she draped Barbara's beautiful quilts over a couple of quilt racks and two folding screens, Devon made sure to not look toward the front of the store where Cole was talking and laughing with the two women. Her jaw clenched at the sound of the women laughing in that way some women had when they liked a guy.

"So, my brother says you've been going out?"

Her attention shot to Cooper while her mind stumbled over possible responses. "Um, just fake dating, to get my mom off my case for a while."

"Uh-huh." He didn't sound convinced. Had Barbara brought him over to her cause? And when did rodeo cowboys become matchmakers? Seriously, there had to be something in the air in Blue Falls. You'd think the place was called True Love Falls or something.

The sound of the door opening again caused her to look toward the front of the store, hoping it was the too-appreciative women leaving. Instead, she saw her mother standing just inside the entrance with a stunned look on her face and Cole nowhere to be seen. Had he left with the women?

Devon resisted the sudden need to scream. That would be a bad move considering her store was full at the moment.

With her stomach knotting more with each step, she headed toward her mother.

"Mom, what can I do for you?"

"I started to call you this morning but I didn't know if you'd pick up."

Devon wanted to tell her that she probably wouldn't have, but she stayed quiet.

"Your father and I are having a party to launch the new line," she said. "I wanted to invite you."

"I don't know. I'm so busy with the Arts and Crafts Trail beginning soon and the holidays around the corner."

"Please, it's only one evening."

The "please" caused Devon to pause. She could probably count on one hand the number of times her mother had said "please" when requesting something of her. More typically the requests hadn't been requests at all, but rather demands.

"Okay, I'll try."

"Good. I'll leave you to…" Her mother gestured vaguely toward all the people in the store.

Again the front door opened, and Cole stepped inside with an apologetic look on his face. He came to stand by Devon and draped his arm casually around her shoulders.

"Hello, Mrs. Newberry. Nice of you to stop by to support Devon's anniversary celebration."

"Uh, oh, yes. Devon, I'll talk to you later." With that, her mother made a hasty exit.

Devon just stared at the door even after it closed behind her mother.

"You okay?" Cole asked.

"Yeah, I've just never seen my mother stumble over her words before."

"I have that effect on women."

Devon laughed then forced herself to step away from his warmth. "That why you disappeared? Sharing your irresistible charm with the tourists?"

"Must have worked. I just booked a commissioned piece."

"That's great!" Before thinking, Devon pulled Cole into a hug. Only when his arms came around her did she realize it had been a bad idea, because she didn't want him to ever let go. Had anything ever felt so good?

Doing her best to keep from letting him see how the hug had affected her, she stepped back and slipped her hands into her pants pockets.

"Though I suspect it has more to do with your artistic talent than your charm."

"So I'm not charming?"

Devon looked up and his gaze captured hers, threatening to steal her ability to breathe, to think coherently, to even ponder her life without him in it.

"I didn't say that. But I doubt all the charm in the world would sell a commissioned piece if your work were butt ugly."

This time, Cole laughed. "I don't think you'd be displaying it in front of your store if it were butt ugly."

"There you go again, making a valid point."

"You can stop flirting now. Your mom is gone," Cooper said, startling Devon with his nearness.

"Zip it," Cole said quietly so no one other than the three of them could hear.

Cooper chuckled as he left the store.

"I'm sorry," Cole said.

"It's okay," Devon said.

"I've always known he can be a pest, but it seems to be getting worse with age."

Devon smiled. "Just be thankful you have a brother. I've always wondered what it would be like to have a sibling."

"I'll sell you mine."

She swatted him on the arm. "I've got to get back to work."

"See you tomorrow."

A thrill went through Devon at the thought of their impending canoe ride. "I'll bring some snacks."

"I'll bring my charming personality."

"Oh, get out of here."

Cole gave her a mischievous smile as he left that made her tingle all over, so much so she feared everyone in the store could feel it, too.

DEVON SAT IN her car in the parking lot next to the lake, taking slow, deep breaths. Even though she and Cole had spent quite a bit of time together and always seemed to have a good time, this felt different. If things suddenly got awkward, there would be no escape from a canoe in the middle of Blue Falls Lake.

She yelped when someone pecked on her window. When she looked out, there stood Cole smiling back at her.

Well, no backing out now.

She stepped out of the car. "Way to give a girl a heart attack."

"You looked like you were going to abandon me. Can't have that. Wouldn't be anywhere near as fun paddling around the lake by myself."

"Just wondering whether I want to entrust my life to you. I have no idea if you're good with a canoe."

"Fair."

"Well, that makes me feel loads better."

Dr. Chloe Kelley stepped to the microphone atop the small stage next to the lake. "Good morning, everyone. Glad to see we have such a big crowd today. The entry fees from this event really do help people in need." After a round of applause, she continued. "And we've added a fun, new element this year. As a surprise for participants, you'll find several small balloons floating around the lake. Each one has a piece of paper inside listing a prize you've won if you capture that balloon, everything from a free lunch at the Primrose to…a weeklong vacation in Hawaii!"

More applause rang through the air.

"Before you board your canoes, feel free to pick up one of these fliers that list all the prizes available. And if you get a chance, be sure to thank the wonderful sponsors who've donated the prizes."

Cole looked over at Devon. "I could always use a free lunch."

"Lunch, smunch, I'm already envisioning myself on the beach in Hawaii."

Cole smiled. "What if it's a trip for two?"

Devon's heart thumped extra hard at the idea of a romantic getaway with Cole.

Stop thinking that way!

"Then Mandy is going to love me more than she already does."

"Is that any way to treat your fake boyfriend?"

She put her forefinger against her chin and pretended to think. "Depends on how fast you paddle that canoe."

"You'll think you're in a motorboat."

She laughed as she grabbed the basket of snacks she'd brought.

It wasn't exactly like a motorboat, but Cole proved how strong he was from years of riding bulls and working on a ranch as he paddled powerfully across the lake. Devon had to keep reminding herself she was supposed to be paddling as well instead of resisting looking over her shoulder to admire Cole's biceps bulging with each pull of his paddle through the water.

But honestly, who could blame her? The man was physical perfection, temptation incarnate. It was a good thing they weren't in a rowboat instead. Then she'd be facing him, making her task of ignoring that physical perfection even more difficult. Whom was she kidding? It'd be impossible.

She dragged her attention away from thoughts of the man behind her as they steered up next to a pink balloon.

"Grab it," he said without breaking stride.

She placed her paddle crossways in front of her and

snatched the balloon as they passed. With nothing sharp to pop the balloon, she squeezed it instead. The piece of paper dropped into her lap.

"What did we win?"

She opened the paper. "Free pizza from Gia's."

"Sound good to me."

She slipped the paper into her pocket and they paddled some more, grumbling when they barely lost another balloon to Nathan and Grace Teague then laughing when they heard the prize was a night's stay at the Teague family's guest ranch.

All across the lake, Devon heard laughter and yelps of victory when someone captured a balloon. "This was a great way to make this more fun."

"What, just spending the day with me wasn't fun enough?"

She waved dismissively. "You're old hat now."

"Be careful. I'll dump you in the lake."

She turned just enough to make eye contact and gave him a stern look. "Don't you dare. Remember, I know where you live."

He just smiled back, a bit of the mischief in his eyes that she'd seen in his brother's.

As they allowed the canoe to float unaided, Devon opened the bag of snacks. "Want something to eat?"

"What do you have?"

"Cheese sticks, crackers, grapes, strawberries, little chicken salad sandwiches."

"I'll take some grapes."

As she pulled them from the bag and once again turned enough to hand him the fruit, he opened his mouth wide.

"Are you serious?"

"Let's see how good your aim is," he said.

"Okay, remember you asked for this." She tossed one of the grapes at him, only to see it bounce off his forehead and into the lake. Devon couldn't help snorting.

Cole laughed. "That snort will have the guys lining up to Fredericksburg to date you."

"Hey! Just for that..." She threw another grape at him, aiming between his eyes. But this time, he snatched it out of the air with his mouth.

He waggled his eyebrows. "Impressed?"

"You got lucky."

"Oh, yeah? Try it again."

She tossed another and again he caught it. Same with the next two.

"Okay, fine, so you have a hidden talent for catching flying fruit."

"I'm a man of many talents."

Devon's body heated at the idea of what some of those unknown talents might be. An image of him stretching out beside her naked made her consider dumping herself in the lake. She shifted her gaze away from him and faced fully forward. In some vegetation near the shore, a balloon floated.

"Hey, there's another balloon." She pointed toward it, then picked up her paddle to help him maneuver the canoe that direction.

When they reached the green balloon, its color helping to hide it, she pulled it aboard as Cole began to back them away from the shore.

"What do you think we'll get this time? Free tire rotation at the service station?" she asked.

"Don't knock it. I think my truck's about due for that."

As Cole glanced behind him toward the middle of the lake, she took the opportunity to watch him. Man, those arms were perfection. She imagined them bracing him above her as they made love.

When Cole started to turn his head back toward her, she jerked her attention to the balloon and popped it. The breeze caught the paper and she barely snatched it before it blew away, leaving them to wonder what the prize had been. The canoe rocked a little with her effort.

"Careful," Cole said. "I can pay for my own tire rotation."

"Yeah, but I'm still hoping for that Hawaiian vacation."

"I still think I should be able to go with you since I'm the one pulling us around this lake."

"Hey, I've been paddling, too."

He grinned. "If that's what you want to call it."

"You sure are in a mood today."

"It's a beautiful day. Good company. I won some pizza."

"*We* won some pizza."

Devon rolled her eyes and looked down as she opened the piece of paper.

"Oh, my God!"

"What's wrong?" Cole asked, his tone changing instantly to one of concern.

She read the paper again to make sure then looked back at him. "The Hawaii trip. Cole, it's the Hawaii trip." She was so excited, she jumped up before she remembered she was in a canoe.

"No!" Cole said as he reached for her.

Devon squealed as the canoe rocked, knocking her off balance. She tried to regain her seat, but it was too late. In the next moment the canoe tipped over, dumping her into the water.

For a moment, Devon panicked as she fell below the

surface of the water. She flailed, her mind trying to figure out which way was up. Just as she spotted the sunlight on the surface, something grabbed her. Without thinking, she opened her mouth to scream in the same moment she was tugged upward.

She broke the surface coughing out lake water, and it took several seconds for her mind to calm enough to recognize that it had been Cole who'd dragged her to the surface of the lake.

"Are you okay?" he asked as he pushed the soaked hair away from her eyes and mouth.

After another cough, she nodded. It took a few more seconds for her breathing to slow. But then it threatened to speed up again when she felt how closely she was pressed to Cole's body. She looked up into his eyes and saw a spark of something there, almost like the last bit of resistance being snuffed out.

In the next moment, he lowered his mouth to hers with a growl that set her blood on fire. The way she'd been pretending with him evaporated, and she lifted her hands to his shoulders and kissed him back. Her head swam with how intoxicating he felt. His strong arms wrapped around her back were like nothing she'd ever felt, as if nothing in her life could ever feel better.

His tongue slipped inside her mouth, and she welcomed it with her own.

She had no idea how long they kissed. The sun could have set while they kissed and treaded water and she wouldn't have noticed. Eventually, they broke apart, both of them breathing hard. He stared down at her as if he couldn't quite believe what had just happened.

Please, don't regret it.

"Way to go, Cole! Looks like you won the big prize out here today."

They both jerked their attention to where Greg Boze man was paddling by, a smiling woman Devon didn't recognize accompanying him. Greg was the poster boy for playing the field, so the lack of recognition wasn't surprising.

Devon wondered if she should move away from Cole, but she didn't want to. She feared she might do something embarrassing like whimper if they broke contact. Of course they couldn't stay in the water the rest of the day, would have to manage getting themselves back into the canoe, but she wasn't ready to let go just yet.

Greg laughed as he moved his canoe farther away.

"I'm sorry about tipping the canoe," she said when Cole returned his attention to her.

"It was a softer landing than I'm used to."

"Oh, your back! You didn't hurt yourself, did you?"

Cole ran his thumb across her cheek, causing her heart to speed up again. "I'm fine. Which is more than I can say for your snack basket." He nodded behind her.

She looked back, still holding on to his arms. The lightweight basket floated upside down, its contents probably at the bottom of the lake.

"Oh, no! The Hawaii prize." Tears popped into her eyes that she'd lost it. She wouldn't be able to claim it, not without proof.

"You mean this?"

She looked back at Cole to see him holding a sodden piece of paper, the first three letters of "Hawaii" all she could read because of the paper being folded over on itself.

"Isn't there a saying about possession being nine-tenths of the law?"

Her mouth dropped open, but how could she deny him? He'd just dragged her to the surface of the lake, made sure she was okay, then given her the best kiss of her life.

He laughed. "I'm joking." He took her hand and placed the wet piece of paper in it, then closed her fingers over the top of it. "What do you say we get out of the water before we turn into prunes?"

He had a point, but a part of her couldn't help wondering what he'd thought of the kiss. It almost seemed as if he was pretending it hadn't happened. Was she that bad of a kisser?

Ugh. Dating, even fake dating, was so complicated.

They grabbed the canoe and swam with it closer to shore to make it easier to climb back in, grabbing the floating paddles along the way. As Cole held her hand while she stepped back into the canoe, it felt as if every tiny bit of her brain was focused on the sensation of their skin touching. She hated to let him go. And once they were back in the canoe, a swamping sense of awkwardness hit her. Thankfully they weren't facing each other or he'd no doubt be able to read her feelings like a large-print book.

"I think we're going to need that pizza when we get back," Cole said from behind her.

"Yeah, considering all the food I brought is feeding the fish right now."

The entire way to the starting point, Cole said nothing about the kiss. Did he not know what to say, or was he hoping she'd just forget about it? As if that was possible. The sudden need to put distance between them, to try to convince herself the kiss had meant nothing to her, made her fidgety.

"You okay?" Cole asked.

"Yeah. Just tired. I suppose a busy week of work and falling in a lake will do that to a gal."

She wondered if he believed her.

Cole jumped out of the canoe when her end moved into the shallow water next to the shore. He extended his hand toward her, and she couldn't refuse to take it without making it obvious how much turmoil was whirling inside her.

When she had two feet on land, Cole didn't release her hand. What was going on? Was it possible his feelings toward her were changing?

"Looks like you two had an eventful ride," Chloe said as she spotted them.

"Yeah, we took an unexpected swim," Devon said.

"Devon was a bit excited by what she found in her balloon." Cole squeezed her hand again, making her pulse snap to attention.

She pulled the wet pieces of paper from her pocket and found the one that had led to her current soggy state.

"Congratulations!" Chloe said when she saw what it said. "Hawaii is so romantic." She gave Cole and Devon a knowing look.

Was it possible Devon could take the dream trip with her dream man?

"I suspect you want to get into something dry, so I'll email you all the details about the trip."

"Okay, thanks."

Cole held her hand all the way back to her car. She hated to let it go, but he stepped aside as she pulled her keys from her pocket.

"Thank goodness these didn't end up at the bottom of the lake," she said as she shook her keys, feeling so nervous she was afraid it was visible. From the moon.

"Congratulations on your trip. You deserve it."

"Whatever for?"

"You work hard, are kind to people."

"So are you."

"I'm just a has-been rodeo cowboy. What would I do on a beach?"

"Soak up the sun like everyone else?"

He gestured toward the sky. "Plenty of sun right here."

She clamped down on saying anything further, not wanting to look desperate.

"Well, I don't know about you, but I think I have some dry clothes at home calling my name. Thanks for coming and doing this today. Rain check on the pizza?"

She nodded, though it seemed they were back to the friend zone, as if that hot kiss out on the lake hadn't happened. Had she knocked her head on the canoe and imagined the whole thing?

"Uh, yeah, no problem. It was fun."

When he leaned forward, she thought maybe she'd misread his distance, that he was going to continue what he'd started out in the middle of the lake. But when he planted a kiss on her cheek instead, her heart sank so hard and fast that she had to bite her lip to keep it from trembling.

As she watched him walk away, it felt so final, as if it might be for the last time.

Chapter Eleven

What the hell had he been thinking? It was all kinds of stupid to start something with Devon because he knew what she was looking for, and he wasn't it. But he hadn't been able to stop himself, not with her pressed so close against him. He tried to pinpoint when the pretend had started being not so pretend, but it had been so gradual, he couldn't. There wasn't one thing he disliked about Devon, and he knew that was bad news. He had to keep his distance. Maybe with her trying online dating, that would hold off her mother.

Besides, he needed to focus on work, especially now that he had a commission to complete.

As he pulled into the ranch, this was one time he wished he lived alone. He couldn't let his mom and brother know what had happened with Devon. His mom would be convinced she'd been right about them all along.

But he was drenched, and soaking-wet underwear wasn't the best-feeling thing ever.

Cooper was headed toward the barn when Cole got out of his truck. His brother started laughing as soon as he saw Cole. "The idea is to stay in the canoe."

"Really? I had no idea."

By the look on his mom's face when he stepped into

the house, he knew word of what happened had already reached her through the miracle speed of the Blue Falls gossip network.

"I'm so happy," she said.

"That your oldest son nearly drowned?" He toed off his sneakers, thankful he hadn't worn his boots for the canoe ride. As it was, the sneakers were going to stink so much they'd have to go in the garbage.

"You swim like a fish," she said. "Have since you were little. You know very well what I mean."

"And you're getting your hopes up for no reason."

"So you didn't kiss Devon?"

"I was just glad she was okay. I didn't know if she could swim."

"So if you'd saved anyone else, you would have kissed them the same way?"

"Depends."

His mom made an exasperated sound. "Why are you resisting your obvious attraction to her so much?"

He spun toward his mom. "Because she wants happily-ever-after. I can't give her that."

"Why not? Maybe she's the one you've been moving toward all along."

He sighed and shook his head. "I don't know what else to tell you. I'm going to take a shower."

She mercifully didn't say anything else as he retreated to the bathroom and fought his way out of his wet clothes and dumped them on the tile floor. He stepped into the shower, intent on washing the events of the day away. Instead, his thoughts went back to that moment he'd stopped resisting and given in to the attraction to Devon that he'd been fighting.

And it had been awesome. When they had walked the same halls of Blue Falls High School, the thought that she'd be a great kisser, that she hid a killer body under all those loose-fitting clothes, had never entered his mind. But since he'd held her and kissed her, it was all he could think about.

The scariest part? He wanted to do it all over again. And maybe more.

No, no *maybe* about it.

He had to stay away from Devon and let her move on with her life, to protect her. To protect himself.

But thinking it and actually doing it were two entirely different things.

DEVON TRIED WORKING on A Good Yarn's website, then restocking the fabric section of the store, and finally rearranging the storeroom. Nothing took her mind off missing Cole. It'd been three days since their outing at Canoe Fest, since the dump into the lake, since their brain-scorching kiss. She'd heard not a peep out of him since, and she hadn't reached out to him, either. If he wanted to step away for good, then she'd let him. He'd told her plain as day he didn't want a serious relationship ever again, and yet she'd allowed herself to hope he might change his mind. No one was to blame but her.

She realized she'd been staring at the display of oatmeal soap for who knew how long when the front door opened. Her brows furrowed when Mandy walked in, followed by India Parrish, who owned Yesterwear Boutique a few doors down, and Skyler Bradshaw, who owned the Wildflower Inn, which overlooked the lake.

"Hey, what are you doing here?" she asked Mandy as she walked toward the front. "It's your day off."

"I came to cheer you up, and I brought reinforcements."

She'd told Mandy everything, including the fact that

she had to find a way to get past the empty feeling inside her.

"I'm fine."

Mandy gave her a look that said she knew good and well Devon was lying.

"You haven't been yourself this week," India said. "You're normally chipper and smiling, but when I passed you yesterday, you looked on the verge of tears."

Devon didn't want to share what a fool she'd been with anyone else, but she had to bite her lip and blink several times to prevent the very tears India had mentioned.

India rubbed Devon's arm. "What's wrong?"

Devon sighed and sank into one of the wicker chairs in the front corner opposite the checkout counter. Her friends sat in the other three chairs that were there for the local knitters' club when they had meetings.

"Is this about Cole?" Skyler asked. "You two looked so happy at the Canoe Fest."

"We were, but...it's not what you think." She glanced toward the ceiling, embarrassed by the words she hadn't yet spoken. "Cole and I have been pretending to date so my mom would stop shoving 'suitable men' toward me."

"Pretending?" Skyler said. "From what Greg says, you guys weren't putting on a show for anyone when you kissed out in the lake. He said you appeared to have forgotten anyone was within miles."

"That...was different. We'd never taken it that far." She paused, thinking back to the kiss, wondering how she'd misinterpreted it.

"Maybe his feelings changed," India said.

Devon shook her head. "Cole has no interest in me."

"I doubt he goes around kissing women he has no interest in," Mandy said, the same as she had when Devon had first told her about the kiss.

"Trust me, it was just a fluke. When we returned to shore, it was as if it hadn't happened. And I haven't heard from him since."

"Do you want there to be more between you?" India asked.

Devon thought about it for a minute before nodding. "But he doesn't. He knows that I'm looking for a happily-ever-after, and he no longer believes in them."

"Then change his mind," Skyler said.

"I don't know if that's possible. He's been married twice, and neither time ended well."

"If you care about him, I think it's worth a try," India said. "Take it a day at a time. But it may require you making the next move."

"You have no idea how much that scares me. If it blows up in my face, I'll still have to see him around town. I can't just disappear into the crowd of a city."

Mandy leaned forward. "Which will be worse, that or never knowing if there could have been more between you? What if there could be and you never find out?"

Devon ran her fingers back through her hair, wondering if there was one sliver of hope she and Cole could have a real relationship. Could he see her as more than a friend? More than the chubby girl from high school he'd overlooked in favor of the girl who'd ended up hurting him? "I feel like I'm going to throw up."

India patted Devon's knee. "It'll be okay. We'll all help you any way we can."

Even after her friends left, Devon couldn't decide whether asking Cole out was a good idea or not. She paced the store for close to an hour before she remembered her mother inviting her to the launch party.

Maybe she'd ask Cole to go to the party with her and see where the night led.

When she picked up her phone to call him, she didn't think she'd ever shaken so much in her life. It was insane to place so much importance on the outcome of one phone call, but she couldn't seem to help it. She'd fallen for Cole, and if those feelings were unrequited she didn't look forward to the process of grieving that, of trying to get past it.

"Hello?"

His voice startled her so much she almost dropped her phone.

"Cole, hi. How's it going?" Good grief, could she sound any more like she was forcing boundless cheer into her response?

"Good. Working on the commissioned piece."

"Oh, that's good."

When she paused too long, he asked, "Something I can do for you?"

"Actually, yes. I hate to ask, but I was wondering if maybe you'd accompany me to a party my parents are hosting, a company thing?"

He didn't answer at first, which caused the nausea to swirl inside her again.

"When is it?"

"Tomorrow night."

"Okay, sure. I'll meet you there."

She tried not to fixate on the last part of his response, on how it sounded like he was trying to make sure she knew this was a favor for a friend and nothing more.

"Great. See you then."

When she hung up the phone after giving him the details, her mind started to race. If she wanted him to know how she felt, to see if there was any chance he could feel the same, she had to commit totally to this one shot. With that in mind, she dialed another number.

"Yesterwear Boutique."

"Hi, India. It's Devon." She paused for a moment. "I need your help."

DEVON PAUSED OUTSIDE the entrance to her parents' gorgeous home, the house where she'd grown up. She smoothed her hand over the front of the green, form-fitting dress, hoping she looked as good as India, Skyler, Elissa and Mandy had told her she did. She couldn't remember ever wearing something so snug, that showed off her true shape. She'd spent so many years hiding under billowy clothing that she'd actually been shocked when she looked in the mirror in India's shop. She'd liked what she saw. Now she just hoped that Cole did, as well.

She made her way inside and almost immediately came face-to-face with her mother.

"Devon, you came." She looked at Devon's ensemble, from her updo down to her heels.

"Do I pass inspection?"

"You look nice. And there's no need to be snippy."

Well, this evening was going great so far.

Her mother steered her through the crowd before Devon could stop her.

"There's someone I want you to meet."

"Mom, I have a date tonight."

Her mother stopped and looked at her. "Cole Davis?" She looked back toward the door. "Well, where is he? He couldn't accompany you inside like a proper gentleman? I guess I shouldn't be surprised."

"Stop it. We agreed to meet here. He'll be here soon."

"Uh-huh." Her mother looked past her and smiled. "Oh, there you are. Just who we were looking for."

A nice-looking young man in an expensive suit stepped up to them holding a drink.

"Devon, dear, this is Christopher Aldridge. He's the governor's nephew. Christopher, this is my daughter, Devon."

Though Devon wanted nothing more than to retrace her steps back outside to call Cole and have him meet her somewhere else, she instead put on a polite smile and shook Christopher's hand. "It's nice to meet you."

"Why don't you two dance?" her mother said.

Before Christopher could move to escort Devon to the dance floor, Devon intervened.

"I'm sorry, but could you excuse me? I need to go meet my date for the evening." She extricated herself from the conversation without even sparing her mother a glance.

Please, Cole, be here already.

But as she crossed the room and looked first toward the entrance and then at all the faces around her, she didn't see him. By the time she'd spent half an hour looking for him and avoiding contact with her parents, she feared she'd been stood up. It didn't seem like Cole to do that to her, even if he was pulling away, but there were no messages on her phone and no sign of him.

She got herself a glass of wine and made small talk with a few of the people she knew from her parents' company, all the while keeping watch for Cole. If he didn't arrive soon, she was going to sneak out and go home. Part of her wanted to go be a hermit at her farm, but she had a business to run. A life to live, the same as she did before Cole Davis came back to town and made her start wishing for things that couldn't be.

After a short conversation with the CFO of Diamond Ranch Western Wear, she unfortunately made eye contact with her mother. The look of smug satisfaction on her mother's face was the last straw. Devon could hear her mother's thoughts as clearly as if the woman had spoken them over a microphone.

I told you he wasn't good enough for you. I told you that you'd regret getting involved with the likes of him.

Devon couldn't stand it anymore. She didn't care if it looked like she was running away because that was exactly her plan when she turned toward the front door... and saw Cole standing there in a dark suit and even a tie. He took her breath away.

When he spotted her, he smiled and headed in her direction. She would not let him know that she'd been about to leave, that she'd thought he'd stood her up.

"I'm sorry I'm so late," he said as he reached her. "What do they call it? A fashion emergency?"

She laughed. "Never thought I'd hear those words come out of your mouth."

"Seems the only suit I owned was no longer the right size. And Mom told me in no uncertain terms that I wasn't showing up here in Western wear, though I think she kind of liked the idea of the look on your mom's face if I did."

"It truly would have been the highlight of the night."

"I should have texted you, but I didn't think it would take so long to get here. Traffic coming back from Austin was terrible, though. Not used to having to think about rush hour."

Up close she could see that the tie he wore was a deep blue with a bit of shimmer in it.

"Well, the trip was worth it. You look very nice."

He took her hands, making her heart leap, and lifted them out to her sides. "And you look gorgeous."

Heat rushed to her cheeks. "Thank you. I might have had a bit of help, as well."

"You don't need help to look beautiful, Devon."

Her heart fluttered and her breath caught as she looked up at him and saw interest in his eyes. She knew she wasn't making it up as part of her wishful thinking.

"May I have this dance?" he asked as the band started playing another song.

She nodded and allowed him to lead her into the marble-floored conservatory, which had been cleared out for the party. When he pulled her close, she decided all the work that had gone into getting ready for this party had definitely been worth it. She didn't know where they'd go after this night, possibly nowhere, but in this moment, she felt like a princess dancing in the arms of her prince.

"I'm sorry I haven't called you," he said. The rumble of his voice vibrated through her.

"No reason to," she said, trying to sound more casual than she felt.

"There was. I kissed you and then ran away like it hadn't happened."

Her heart thumped a bit harder. He'd brought up the kiss. What did that mean?

"I liked it. Too much," he said.

"You did?"

He smiled, and she fell a little more in love with him. Thinking those actual words, giving voice to "love" even if it was only in her head, scared her. It made her too vulnerable.

"Yeah." He lifted his hand and ran his thumb over her cheek. "I wanted to pretend it hadn't happened because I can't give you what you want. I know you want forever, and I didn't want to start something with you when I knew I couldn't give that to you."

"Oh." Did that mean he had feelings but just not ones strong enough to change his mind about commitment?

"Don't get me wrong. I do want you, Devon, but it would have to be casual, no strings. No ring."

Could she agree to that with how she felt about him? Would having him for a little while be better than not having him at all, or would her heart break when he finally called it quits?

Her friends were convinced that she could change his mind, or maybe even make him realize what he was already feeling, that maybe the third time was the charm. Devon wanted that to be true, so much.

Looking up at him, she made a decision. She was going to grab what happiness she could with him. And if it ended at some point, she'd deal with the emotional fallout then.

"Okay."

His forehead scrunched. "Okay?"

"I like you, Cole, and I've been thinking about that kiss nearly nonstop since it happened."

"What are you saying?"

"I'm saying I don't want to pretend anymore."

His grin was slow and just about the sexiest thing she'd ever seen. "Would you be opposed to leaving the party a little early?"

"Not in the least."

A flash of something that she thought was desire shone in his eyes before he took her hand and headed toward the door. Devon noticed her mother heading in their direction.

Devon tugged Cole behind a group of men who were

standing near the bar talking, guiding him out the conservatory's exterior door instead of trying to make her way through the crowd to the front.

"What's the rush?" Cole asked, laughter in his voice.

"My mother was incoming."

She led him around the house through the backyard, but before they could turn the final corner, Cole pulled her to a stop and backed her up against the side of the house.

"And here I thought you were just anxious to be alone with me."

Her heart thumped wildly at the warm length of his body pressed along her front. "That might be part of the equation."

He gave her another one of those devastating smiles before lowering his mouth to hers and kissing her so thoroughly, it put the kiss in the lake to shame.

Devon moaned into his mouth, which seemed to add fuel to the fire that had sprung up between them. Cole's hands slid down the back of her dress to cup her bottom. Potent desire flooded the entirety of her body, and she gripped his upper arms to steady herself.

The sound of voices coming from the backyard worked their way through the haze of desire enveloping her, causing her to push Cole away. "Not here."

"We can't go to my house. Mom is there."

"I don't think my cat will mind if you come to my house."

Though she hated losing contact with him, they drove separately. There was no way she was leaving her car behind at her parents' house, inviting questions she didn't want to answer. As it was, she knew she'd catch her mother's disapproval for leaving so abruptly and without saying goodbye to her parents. Well, if this night ended up the way she thought it might, she could handle anything her mother threw at her.

Devon's nerves danced all the way home. By the time she stepped out of her car next to her house, her legs were shaky with anticipation. Cole parked next to her and didn't waste any time slipping from his truck and making his way to her. He pulled her into a hungry kiss without saying anything.

Was it possible for a person to combust from too much desire? If so, she was definitely on the verge of going up in flames.

"Inside," she managed to say in between kisses.

She led him to the house, grumbling under her breath when she fumbled her keys at the door.

Cole chuckled as he stepped inside behind her. "Flustered?"

"Behave or I can throw you out."

He framed her face between his hands. "You don't want that."

He was right. She didn't.

More kisses followed until Honeysuckle gave an insistent meow, demanding to be paid some attention.

"Sorry, kitty," Cole said. "Your owner is otherwise occupied."

Honeysuckle mewed again, as if saying she didn't think much of his response.

Cole chuckled but when his gaze captured Devon's, all thoughts of the cat or anything other than the man in front of her fled.

He caressed her cheek. "As pretty as that dress is, I'd rather get you out of it. But I want you to be sure, Devon. I want you to know what you're getting."

She ran her hand up his firm chest. "I do."

With that, she led him toward her bedroom.

Chapter Twelve

Devon hoped she didn't pass out from the simultaneous firing of all of her nerves before she could get Cole to her bed. She still couldn't believe he was here, in her bedroom, with her. If this was a dream and she woke up, she was going to be extremely ticked off.

When they reached the edge of the bed, Cole stepped up behind her and dropped his lips to the side of her neck. He worked his way up to her ear and when his tongue flicked the lobe, she grew unsteady on her feet.

Cole chuckled softly in her ear before placing his large hands on her shoulders. "Are you sure about this?"

She couldn't look at him as she nodded, couldn't find the breath to speak a single word.

"Don't be nervous," he said as he began to slowly unzip the back of her dress. "I won't hurt you."

She knew in the end she probably would get hurt, but she shoved those thoughts aside. If she couldn't have forever, she was going to pay attention and savor every moment of this night.

When her dress dropped to the floor, she didn't think she'd felt more vulnerable. Out of instinct, she wrapped her arms around herself. Cole spun her slowly to face him then guided her arms away from where they crisscrossed her front.

"Don't hide yourself, Devon. You're beautiful."

She had no idea what to say to that.

"You don't believe me?"

She shrugged. "I don't know."

He lifted her chin until she was looking into his eyes. "Don't tell me that your mother told you you're not beautiful."

She shook her head. "No. I…I guess I just still feel like…" Her voice faltered before she managed to rein in some small portion of her nerves. "…Like that fat girl from high school."

"You weren't fat."

He couldn't have surprised her more if he'd said he'd wanted to be a cheerleader instead of the star of the rodeo team.

"I must have been better at hiding it than I thought."

Cole took a step closer and framed her face with his hands. "It doesn't matter who either of us was in the past." Then he lowered his mouth to hers and showed her exactly how hungry he was for her.

Something unlocked inside her, a reserve that had always been as much a part of her as her hair or the heart now imitating a revving engine in her chest. She'd planned to take things slowly, luxuriating in every touch, every kiss, every single spot at which Cole's body connected with hers. But a burning need to feel all of him filled her and burst forth.

Her hands went to his suit jacket and shoved it from his shoulders, then to loosening the tie.

"In a hurry?" he asked against her lips.

"Yes."

Her single-word answer seemed to light a fire under Cole's own ardor as he moved to unfasten his belt while she unbuttoned his crisp white shirt. He dropped his pants and kicked off his shoes, leaving him standing in front of her in less than she was wearing. Unwilling to deny herself anything, she ran her hands up and over the hard, toned planes of his chest.

Cole growled low in his throat and lifted her in his arms then stretched her out along the bed. Her heart beat so fast as he stripped her of her underwear and heels that it reverberated throughout her body, banging against the inside of her eardrums to the point she thought she might go deaf.

Cole trailed kisses all over her body, seeming to leave not one inch of skin untouched. Her hands gripped his back, feeling the play of muscles he'd developed from years of riding bulls. She nearly laughed hysterically when the thought passed through her addled brain that soon he was going to be riding her.

She ran her hands down his back to the curve of his hips. Feeling like she was inhabiting someone else's body, she slipped her hands below his underwear and gripped his hips. The length of him pressing against her thigh hardened even more.

Cole didn't say a word as he rolled away to the edge of the bed.

Panic swept through her like a shock wave. Had she gone too far? Or had he changed his mind? If so, she knew she wasn't going to be strong enough to hold back her tears until he left.

But then he pulled off his underwear and bent over to get something. The sound of tearing told her exactly what he'd retrieved, and the center of her body ached in anticipation.

When Cole spread himself alongside her again, she got caught in his gaze and lifted her hand to place it against his cheek. He turned his head to drop a kiss into the center of her palm.

She couldn't believe this was happening, that so many of her fantasies were becoming reality.

As if he could see the answer in her eyes to a question he didn't have to ask, Cole settled himself between her legs, gently spreading them wider. A shiver ran throughout her body.

"Are you okay?" Cole asked.

"Yeah. It's just…"

"What?"

She knew it wasn't her best self-confidence moment, but she didn't want him to be disappointed in their lovemaking. She shook her head.

"Nothing." She ran her hands up his powerful arms and then his neck, twining her fingers through his close-cropped hair and pulling him down to her for a kiss that could say more than words.

His hands gripped her hips as he pressed closer, closer until he slid home. Oh, merciful heavens, that's what it felt like to have him inside her—home. The depth of that feeling should scare her, and it did a little, but it also sent such a well of warmth and rightness coursing through her body that the fear couldn't overcome it.

She rose to meet his thrusts, thrilling at the sounds he was making as he held her close and fed both of their needs. Their mouths made love to each other the same as the rest of their bodies, and gradually their pace increased. The very core of her vibrated, growing closer to release. Cole must have sensed it because he increased his pace even more, sending wave after wave of pleasure through her.

As she reached the verge, she couldn't kiss him anymore and still be able to pull enough oxygen into her lungs. She threw her head back against the pillow and strained upward as Cole made another powerful thrust that sent her over the edge, setting off what felt like an earthquake inside her.

She was still riding the aftershocks when Cole stiffened, his muscles straining, and found his own release. A powerful joy filled her at what they'd just shared, and she had to fight the need to grab on to him and never let him go.

No strings, he'd said, and she'd agreed to it.

Cole collapsed beside her but left one of his legs and his right arm draped over her. She loved the warm weight of them. He pulled her closer to him and smoothed her hair away from her face.

"We should have stopped pretending long before tonight," he said.

Devon smiled, inside and out. Tomorrow, she'd deal with the repercussions of what she'd done, but for now she was going to bask in the happiest moment of her life.

COLE DRIFTED HALFWAY between sleep and being awake. He lifted his heavy eyelids to see Devon lying beside him, still naked and still as beautiful as she'd been when they'd both fallen asleep. As he'd made love to her, he'd been stunned by how beautiful she was, how giving. Of course, he'd known both things, but it was as if being together as they had, it had been magnified a hundredfold.

For a moment, he wished his experiences hadn't ruined him for serious relationships because Devon was the kind of woman who made them seem plausible. But he had been ruined, and there was no going back to change that. He'd been surprised when Devon agreed to a casual relationship for however long it lasted. Surprised, but really glad. With her agreement, he'd been able to stop holding back how his very real attraction to her had been growing every day.

Devon rolled to face him, allowing the sheet to drift lower to show him a tantalizing swell of breast. His mouth watered to taste it again. Smiling, he took a lock of her hair between his fingers and brought it to her nose. Her forehead wrinkled and she rubbed at the tickling.

Unable to help himself, he laughed. The sound woke her, and at first she looked at him with sleep-heavy eyes. It made her all the more sexy, and he grew hard with wanting her again.

"Were you tickling my nose?" she asked, sounding drowsy.

"What will you do if I say yes?"

She sprang on him so fast, he yelped.

"See if you're ticklish." Suddenly, her questing fingers seemed to be everywhere, trying to find his ticklish spot.

Well, he had one, but he would make her work harder than this to find it. Cole rolled her onto her back, pinning her hands above her head on the pillow. He chuckled at her look of frustration.

"Not fair," she said.

"Neither is how beautiful you are when you wake up."

"Oh, now you're just lying. I'm sure I have crazy bed hair and probably pillow creases on my cheeks."

He dropped a soft kiss on her lips. "You need to learn to take compliments better."

She didn't say anything in response, simply looked up at him with a spark of desire flickering in her eyes. "Make love to me again," she whispered.

It was so out of character for her, so tender, so honest that it caused a pang in his chest. But he gave her what she wanted, what they both wanted. It was slow, fulfilling but also…sweet. He wondered if this had been a good idea when he had the thought that he was going to have to guard against really falling for her. Against opening himself up the way he'd sworn he never would again the moment he'd signed the second set of divorce papers.

After they both reached completion, he pulled her close. He told himself not to think about how good it felt to have her there in the crook of his arm, how he could get used to it. He'd learned from his mistakes. This time, he was taking it one day at a time and not thinking about what the next might or might not bring.

"This is nice," Devon said, her warm breath drifting across his chest.

"Yeah, way better than wearing that suit."

She leaned back and looked up at him. "You looked very handsome in that suit." A saucy-looking grin spread her lips. "Though I have to say I also prefer you out of it."

"That right?"

"Yep."

"I feel the same way about your dress."

They kissed some more, then fell into a comfortable, drowsy silence. Though he hated to move away from her soft warmth, he knew he had to.

"I need to go."

"Really?" She seemed to catch herself then pulled away from him. "Oh, right. Your mom."

Something about her reaction tugged on his heart, making him want to pull her close again and not let her go until the sun rose. But she was right. Even though they might really be dating now, he didn't want his mom getting ideas about a wedding and grandbabies. And he might be a grown man, but he still didn't feel right spending the night at a woman's house while he lived under his mother's roof.

Even so, as he slipped from the bed and dressed, aware that Devon was doing the same, a strange sense of wrongness settled on him. Had he made a mistake taking things further with her, knowing that she wanted to get married someday?

Well, she still could. Most likely their relationship would run its course with one or both of them initiating the gradual separation. But unlike most of the other women he'd shared a bed with, he found himself hoping they could remain friends.

Devon slipped from the room as he was tying his shoes. When he stepped into her living room, he spotted her feeding her cat in the kitchen. He leaned on the doorway between the two rooms.

"Is she still ticked off?"

Devon looked up at him and gave him a small smile. It was such a simple, quick expression, but damn if he didn't grow warm inside.

"She's got fresh food and water now. She'll get over it." She scratched the cat's head between the ears. "She knows how good she's got it."

Devon didn't touch him as she accompanied him to the front door. "I had a nice time tonight."

He paused just inside the door and turned her to face him. "Me, too." He ran the backs of his fingers down her silky cheek. "We should do it again sometime."

"I'd like that."

"What do you say to going on a trail ride tomorrow?"

"I have to work."

"Call in sick."

"Um, I own the place."

"Then you can have Mandy work so you can spend the day with a devilishly handsome man."

She smiled, and damn if the light in her eyes didn't make his heart flutter. "Know where I can find one?"

He captured her in his arms and pressed her body close to his. "You're a funny one."

Still hungry for her, he lowered his mouth and savored the feel of hers. He deepened the kiss when she melted into him. Though it nearly killed him, he pulled away and took a single step back.

"See you tomorrow, beautiful."

With a final quick kiss, he stepped out through the door. All the way home, he fought the powerful urge to turn around and find his way back into Devon's bed, into her arms.

DEVON SAT IN her car outside the rear door of A Good Yarn. Though she'd gone over it at least a thousand times in her head, she had no idea what she was going to tell Mandy about what had happened the previous night. Because there was no way Mandy wasn't going to ask. Devon just didn't know whether she should be entirely truthful, especially since she knew that what was between her and Cole would be over sooner or later. It could be over already, as far as she knew, especially after she'd texted him earlier to ask for a rain check on the trail ride. She'd told him she needed to work on some things for the opening of the Arts and Crafts Trail but that she'd call him later to reschedule.

She'd wondered if he'd take it the wrong way, that she was no longer interested in being with him. The reality was that she needed time to find her equilibrium after the previous night. Being in Cole's arms had been... *Ecstasy* was the only word that truly captured how she'd felt.

When it had taken him several minutes to respond, she'd begun to wonder if perhaps he'd satisfied his desire and was already pulling away. He'd texted back eventually, saying he'd been in the shower. The image of water running over that magnificent body of his had caused her core temperature to rise several degrees. He'd teased that he supposed he could find something to do to take his mind off where he'd rather be.

For a moment, the way he'd responded had given her hope for something more. But as she had before agreeing to take the next step with him, she reminded herself it was only temporary. There would come a day when they wouldn't see each other, wouldn't text, at least not as anything more than friends. She certainly hoped their friendship wasn't a casualty of them making things physical.

Well, she'd deal with that when the time came. She'd known going in what she was getting herself into.

She grabbed her purse and made her way inside. As expected, Mandy nearly accosted her when she stepped into the store.

"How did it go? Did he trip over his own feet at how beautiful you were?"

"What, a girl can't even have her morning coffee before she's attacked?"

"I know you had coffee before you left your house this morning," Mandy said. "You would have driven off the road otherwise."

The downside of working with your best friend— she knew everything about you, including your caffeine schedule.

"It was nice," Devon said as she made her way past Mandy toward the front of the store.

"Oh, no. You're not getting by with a throwaway response like that."

Devon stopped at the end of the checkout counter and braced her hands against it. And then she spilled the beans. Every...last...bean.

Mandy squealed in response, a sound so high-pitched Devon was glad the store wasn't open yet and that might have perked up the ears of all the dogs in town.

"How was it?"

Devon gave her friend a deliberately confused look. "It?"

"You know exactly what I mean."

Devon couldn't stop grinning. "It was fantastic. Better than any daydream I've ever had."

Mandy, so excited she appeared to be vibrating, pulled Devon in for a tight hug. "I'm so excited for you."

And that's when reality came crashing down. Devon stepped away from Mandy and took a fortifying breath.

"It doesn't change the fact that Cole doesn't want a serious relationship. We're keeping it casual, and when it's over, it's over."

Mandy just stared at her as if she'd told her the earth was actually shaped like a triangle and humanity was descended from cats. "You agreed to that?"

Devon hesitated a moment before nodding. "I couldn't resist the opportunity to be with him, even if it's not for long. I had this feeling deep in the pit of my stomach that I'd regret it."

"But you won't when he walks away and you're still in love with him?"

Devon wanted to deny she was in love with Cole, but she couldn't.

"I know that will hurt, a lot, but…I want this. I need it."

"Maybe now that you're together for real, he'll change his mind. Work to make him see how good he'd have it with you. You're not the same as the women he's been with before."

Devon took Mandy's hands in hers and gently squeezed. "I won't pressure him into something he doesn't want. I need you to trust me on this, and to let it be."

Mandy looked like she had lots more to say, but she held herself in check.

"Thank you," Devon said.

"I don't like it, and I hate the idea of you opening yourself up to heartbreak like this, but it's your life. I guess you've had enough of people trying to tell you how to live it."

As Mandy moved toward the back of the store to unpack a new shipment of shopping bags with the A Good Yarn logo on them, Devon turned and watched the comings and goings along Main Street. She needed a few minutes to once again bury the worry about how she would get through eventually losing Cole. She'd told Mandy that she wanted to enjoy every moment with Cole to the fullest, and that's exactly what she intended to do.

WHEN DEVON LEFT the store at the end of the day, Cole was leaning against her car. She startled at the sight of him somewhere she hadn't expected. And then her heart soared that he still wanted to see her enough to be there. Throughout the day, she'd mentally coached herself about how to handle every scenario she could think of, including never being near Cole again. She was glad she didn't have to put that particular plan into action.

"You lurk behind stores often?"

Cole smiled and pushed away from the car, then walked lazily toward where she stood.

"Only yours."

When he reached her, he pulled her into his arms then backed her against the wall of the building. His mouth came down on hers, hungry, insistent. The same desire she'd ridden the night before came back just as strong, if not stronger, and she kissed him with everything she had.

"Get a room!"

Devon jerked away from Cole so quickly, she banged her head on the building.

"You okay?" he asked as his hand came up to the side of her head, ready to check for injury.

"Yeah."

The sound of laughter drew her attention down the line of stores. India waved at them as she headed for her own vehicle. Devon's cheeks flamed.

"You know, that's not a half-bad idea," Cole said next to her ear, causing her blush to go critical.

How quickly they'd gone from pretending to heated kisses and desire that burned like wildfire on a parched prairie.

"Open the door," he whispered.

She had to be crazy, but she did exactly as he said. Once they were inside the storeroom and he'd turned the lock behind him, he captured her mouth again and she moaned at the delicious tingling sensation dancing across her skin. Everything happened so fast. One moment they were kissing, and what seemed like the next she was half-naked, sitting astride him while he sat in her cushy chair where she sometimes knitted or worked on the store's books.

When Cole slipped inside her and she began to rock against him, it was as if she was having an out-of-body experience. She'd never known this person lived within her, the wanton who was enjoying the spontaneous, naughty bit of lovemaking. Though she knew Mandy had gone to visit her mom, the small possibility she might walk in and find them was both frightening and thrilling at once.

Good grief, who was she becoming? Or had she been this person all along and never had the opportunity to discover it?

When she finally reached her climax, she cried out. Cole peaked right along with her, and afterward she fell forward into his arms.

"I can't believe we just did that," she said against his neck. "I will die of mortification if someone heard."

Even though she couldn't see his face, she had the distinct impression he was smiling. What they'd just shared was one of those guy badge-of-honor things, she supposed.

"That was way better than a trail ride," he said, a rumble of a self-satisfied chuckle in his chest.

She swatted him. "You are a bad influence."

"Nah. You like it."

She couldn't argue with that because he was right.

Chapter Thirteen

Cole opened the box and pulled out one of the business cards. He shook his head at the image of his now-completed horse sculpture, his name in bold print and his contact information. Never in all the years he'd lived had he imagined he'd be the type of guy with a business card. Not much call for them when you were riding bulls for a living. But if you wanted to get the word out and drum up buyers for your artwork? Yeah, you needed business cards and a website, both of which Devon had helped him create over the past week.

Somehow she'd found time between her own work and his penchant for pulling her into kisses so hot he'd swear he was going to have scorch marks from his lips to his boots.

The past week had been nothing short of awesome. For the first time since he'd returned home after retiring, he truly felt alive again. He had his art, life on the ranch he loved, and looked forward to seeing Devon every day. It didn't matter if they were helping each other prepare for the upcoming weekend's big launch of the Arts and Crafts Trail, eating pizza while sitting by the lake or enjoying each other in bed, she made him smile and forget this wasn't the life path he'd chosen in the first place.

"I like seeing that smile on your face."

He looked up from where he stood on the front porch holding the box of cards to find his mom sitting on the porch swing. He hadn't even noticed her when he'd pulled up. As it tended to be lately, his head was too filled with Devon Newberry.

"Got my new business cards. Looks like I'm all legit." He strode to the swing and handed her a card.

"Very nice. Though that doesn't surprise me." She gave it back to him. "That girl cares a great deal about you."

"We have fun." He had to give his mom something, but not too much. Despite the fact that he and Devon were really dating now, he didn't want his mom thinking that it would lead to something more. They would both eventually move on.

At least that was the plan. Over the past few days, he hadn't wanted to think about that eventuality. But then, no one said it had to be anytime soon. As long they both were having a good time, he didn't see any reason to cut things off.

"I think it's more than that, and you're just too afraid to admit it."

His mom's words had a bit too much ring of truth in them, so much so that it made him antsy and wonder if the whole situation was a mistake.

But how could something that felt so damn good be a mistake?

Not wanting to seem defensive, he simply ignored her comment. "Heard from Cooper this morning. Said he tweaked his knee last night but he's going to power through tonight. He's darn close to making the cutoff for the Finals."

The sigh coming from his mother likely served a

dual purpose—worry that her second son was riding hurt just as his older brother had and the fact that the older brother was totally ignoring her efforts to make him believe he was…what? Falling in love with Devon? He was pretty sure he'd used up his lifetime's allotment of believing that.

"Don't you hurt that girl," his mom said, her voice more stern than before.

"Mom, Devon knows this is a casual thing."

"Does she?"

"Yes." At least she said she did when she'd agreed to dating for real. He had to take her at her word. And if it proved otherwise, well, he'd figure out how to deal with that when and if the time came.

Wanting to abandon this topic altogether, he went to drop the cards and the rest of the mail on the table just inside the door and then headed for the barn. Just in case the Arts and Crafts Trail turned out to be successful and those driving it didn't skip him altogether, he had some tidying up to do.

But after he'd swept out his work area and moved all his sculptures around at least half a dozen times, he realized there was nothing else to do. He was as ready as he was going to get. What he hadn't expected was the feeling of nervousness making it difficult to stand still. If he wanted the art thing to be a legitimate source of income, this weekend needed to go well. If it didn't, he wasn't sure if he could justify putting any more effort into the sculptures. He might piddle for a hobby, but if it became apparent there wasn't a market for his work then he needed to refocus his attention on the ranch and ways of making it more profitable.

But right now, all he wanted to do was go find Devon and kiss the living daylights out of her. The woman was an unexpected but highly addictive drug. When he thought about it, he was surprised she was still single. But maybe her mother's constant efforts to set her up had left little time and opportunity to find someone she actually liked.

He thought of that online dating site where she'd signed up. She hadn't said anything else about it. Had she even gone looking through the profiles? Or had she been too busy with work and dealing with her mother? And with him? He liked the idea of him keeping her mind off all those unknown men, even though that was selfish on his part. She wanted forever with someone, and he was delaying her finding her Mr. Right. But damn, he didn't want to give her up yet.

With that in mind and with everything ready for the opening of the trail the next day, he hopped in his truck and headed to town. When he parked on Main Street, he saw Devon through the window of her shop. She and someone else, probably Mandy, appeared to be doing something over on the side of the store that held the chairs and small table.

With a buzz of anticipation, he got out of the truck and jogged across the street. When he stepped inside the store, she looked up from where she was placing brochures about A Good Yarn on the table.

"About ready for tomorrow?" he asked.

She smoothed back the wisps of her curly hair that had escaped her ponytail. "I think so, though I feel like I'm forgetting something."

"You haven't forgotten anything," Mandy said as she stepped up to the front counter with a few short, fat candles. She quickly arranged them, likely with the intent of encouraging impulse purchases at the register, then looked at him. "She's been worried all day."

"This is important," Devon said.

"And we're ready."

Devon shifted her gaze to Cole. "Why aren't you prepping for tomorrow?"

"Because I'm ready, too. Only so much you can do with metal sculptures displayed in a barn."

"Did the business cards come in?"

He slowly closed the distance between them. "They did, and they look great." He pulled her close.

"Cole, not here."

He grinned at her when he remembered what they'd done in the back room. "Why not?"

"We're open, and I'm running a business here."

He just chuckled before capturing her mouth with his. For someone who had protested his simply holding her in his arms, she sure did fall into the kiss easily. And he took full advantage.

When he finally released her, she looked a little addled for a few seconds before she took a step back and straightened.

"You're a bad influence," she said, half reprimanding, half teasing.

"From where I'm standing, I need a bad influence," Mandy said.

Devon's cheeks flushed red, making Cole smile all the wider.

"Is there anything I can help you with?" he asked.

Devon scanned the store then shook her head. "I think Mandy's right. We're about as ready as we can get. But I bet I don't sleep a wink tonight."

Visions of why she might be awake strolled through his mind. The sound of a snort behind him said that Mandy's mind had gone right to the same place.

Devon put her hands on her hips. "You're both impossible."

"Actually, I'm pretty easy," he said.

Mandy full out laughed at that. "You two need to leave before it really does get not safe for work in here. Go, do couple things."

Couple. He hadn't really thought of him and Devon that way even though they were sleeping together. It sounded more serious than he'd intended, and yet it felt right. And he did want to go do couple things with her. He was surprised when he realized sex wasn't even at the top of the list, though he fully intended for it to be on the night's agenda at some point. But even though their relationship was casual, he wanted more than sex. He could satisfy that itch with any number of women, but what he couldn't get with them was someone he truly liked as a person, someone who was a good listener, willing to help those around her, who seemed to instinctively know so much about him. In the short time they'd really known each other, it felt as if Devon knew him better than either of his wives ever had. Cared about him more than both of them put together.

Something moved in his chest, something that felt like a lot more than casual dating. Oh, hell. He fought the urge to turn and run out the front door. Without him even realizing it, Devon was becoming more important to him than he'd ever expected. The self-preservation part of his brain screamed for him to abort, to bring about the end of their relationship sooner rather than later.

But another part of him, a bigger and growing one, wanted to punch the screaming part in the mouth. Yeah, he cared about Devon. She meant a lot to him, and he liked being with her, but that didn't mean it had to end in wedding bells.

"You okay?" Devon asked.

Damn, how long had he been standing there with his thoughts racing?

"Yeah. How about that trail ride I was promised?"

Looked like today wasn't going to be the day he pulled away for good.

DEVON WAS CONFLICTED when they reached a lovely sloping meadow on the Teagues' guest ranch. On the one hand, she was more than ready to get off the horse and stretch her legs, to explore the beauty of the spot. But that would mean leaving the nice, warm nook in front of Cole. She tried not to think about it, but in the back of her mind she always knew that each day with him could be the last. That wasn't a great way to live, always with a layer of dread accompanying her everywhere she went, but it was the situation in which she found herself.

She'd considered ending their relationship first to protect herself, but that felt like an overreaction. She was strong, more than just what a man made her, so she would survive whatever heartache was to come. In the meantime, she wanted to enjoy her time with him and not regret it when it was over.

"You're awfully quiet," Cole said, the vibration of his voice rumbling through his chest behind her.

"Just appreciating the view."

"Nathan told me about it. I thought it sounded like a place you'd enjoy."

"It's so quiet and peaceful. Makes you realize just how much noise there is even in a town as small as Blue Falls."

"That's one of the things I missed when I was still

on the circuit," he said. "Being able to ride out across the pastures and not hear anything that wasn't part of Mother Nature."

Cole dismounted then reached up for her. She swung her leg over the saddle and sank down into his arms. When she looked up into his eyes to find him watching her with appreciation that she felt all the way to her marrow, she lifted to her tiptoes and kissed him. He reciprocated in the most delicious way, causing the meadow and the world beyond it to fade away.

When they finally drifted out of the kiss, her heart was thumping like a runaway jackhammer in her chest. To keep her thoughts from latching on to words such as *forever* and *happily-ever-after*, she forced humor into her voice as she said, "Well, that doesn't get old."

Cole laughed. "No, it doesn't."

He slid his hand down her arm and entwined his fingers with hers, then led her away from where he left his horse to graze. They didn't speak as they walked through the meadow, and it was actually surprisingly nice. Calm, peaceful, easy. No longer paying her silent command any heed, her thoughts created images of her and Cole walking through this same meadow, holding hands, with rings on their fingers and a couple of adorable children chasing butterflies up ahead of them. An intense longing hit her square in the chest, so powerful she had to resist the urge to rub away the ache.

"You look like you're miles away," Cole said as he squeezed her hand.

"Sorry. Just thinking how lucky I am. Good friends, a business I love, living in a place that's so beautiful. A gal couldn't ask for more."

Except having the man she loved love her back.

Cole directed them to a spot near the top of the

meadow and sat. She followed, sitting close beside him. He continued to hold her hand, and it felt so natural, as if they'd had years of practice.

"You're right," he said. "We're pretty darn lucky."

He didn't elaborate, and she didn't allow herself to do it for him.

They talked a bit about the weekend's opening of the Arts and Crafts Trail and spent a few minutes watching a couple of deer at the lower edge of the meadow. Devon found herself never wanting to leave this little slice of Eden.

"You're beautiful."

The unexpected compliment from Cole drew her attention to him. He actually looked startled that he'd said it out loud, but the intensity in his gaze made her want to believe it. Instead, she smiled and said, "I think you've been out in the sun too long."

"Why do you do that?"

"What?"

"Brush off compliments."

She shrugged. "I don't know. Maybe they just don't feel truthful."

His expression tightened. "You think I'm lying to you?"

She turned part of the way toward him. "No, it's not that. It's just that… Well, it feels like you're not really seeing me."

Cole lifted his hand to the side of her head and slid his thumb across her temple. "I see you clear as day. And despite banging my noggin on the ground who knows how many times, I still have pretty good eyesight."

She smiled a little, but echoes of the past still asserted themselves.

"Did someone tell you that you're not beautiful?" Cole asked. "Your mom?" He'd asked her that before, and that he asked again made her suspect he realized it did indeed have to do with her mother.

"Not in so many words. It's just…" A lump formed in her throat and she turned back to face the meadow. She considered changing the subject, but the truth churned in her stomach. "I guess you could say I tried to eat my way out of my unhappiness as a teenager. It's why I wore the baggy, shapeless clothes. My mom was so unaware of how the pressure she put on me to be perfect chipped away at my self-esteem. I remember she bought me an outfit for one of the big Christmas parties the company hosted, and it was three sizes too small. I couldn't face talking to her about it, so I acted like I was sick that night so I could stay in bed."

Cole was quiet for so long that she chanced a glance his direction, hoping she didn't see disgust on his face. Instead, she saw the telltale signs of anger. Tightened jaw. Stiff posture. Heightened color.

"You have no idea how much I want to go give your mom a huge piece of my mind right now."

His words, the way he said them, the righteous anger on her behalf, touched something so deep and profound in her that she fell the rest of the way in love with him. She couldn't help it, even if she'd tried with every ounce of her strength. This time, she was the one to place her hand against his cheek.

"It wouldn't change anything, but thank you for the sentiment." She paused for a moment as he turned his head and kissed her palm. "You probably don't remember this, but you actually did stand up for me once, with Amy."

"I did?"

She nodded. "She was making fun of me, and you told her to stop. That was it, but you have no idea how much I appreciated it." She left out how even then she'd felt something for him. No need to make their eventual parting more awkward than it was already likely to be.

"I'm sorry I was a lot more clueless then."

"It was high school. We were all clueless."

"You weren't."

"Trust me there were lots of things I was completely clueless about." Such as how to make her mother accept her for who she was, not who her mother wanted her to be. Some things never changed.

As the afternoon waned toward evening, she glanced over at where the horse was leisurely munching. "Shouldn't we head back before it gets dark?"

"Nah. I thought we'd watch the stars come out."

Did he have any idea how romantic that sounded?

And it was. They lay back in the grass and watched as the heavens seemed to turn on one star after another until the entire dark expanse of the sky was covered with them. Between the heavenly beauty, the soft breeze and the warm, reassuring feel of Cole's hand wrapped around hers where they lay on the grass between them, Devon didn't think she could have created a more perfect way to spend her evening.

If only it could last forever.

COLE SANK DOWN onto a hay bale and gulped half a bottle of water. When he'd agreed to have his art be part of the Arts and Crafts Trail, he figured he could always pull out if no one showed up. He couldn't have been more surprised by the steady stream of art lovers who'd not only found their way to the ranch but who'd either bought something or commissioned pieces from him. His buddies still riding the rodeo circuit would get a kick out of it, but a sense of accomplishment filled him that he hadn't truly felt since his days of winning rodeo buckles.

He pulled out his phone and texted Devon about his latest commission and to see how things were going at the shop.

That's awesome! she texted back after a couple of minutes. We're full to the gills here.

He imagined her chatting with customers, her smile ensuring they'd come back as much as her products. Damn, he'd grown to love that smile. Anything to do with Devon, really. Lying in that meadow with her looking up at the stars had been about as perfect an evening as he could ever remember having.

He shook his head. He'd sworn to himself he'd never be serious about a woman again, but Devon was making it really hard to keep that promise. When he wasn't with her, he couldn't seem to go five minutes without thinking about her. He kept trying to tell himself to retreat, that he didn't want to walk this path again, but it didn't feel true anymore. Something deep in his gut told him that Devon was nothing like Amy or Bridget. And that was a good thing because he suspected he was falling for her.

No, there was no suspicion about it. He was certain.

"You must be thinking about Devon."

He'd been so lost in his thoughts that he hadn't heard his mom's approach. He was coming to the conclusion that she was either stealthy or he was really unaware.

"What makes you say that?"

"The look on your face. You love that girl. And don't bother denying it."

His instinct was to do exactly that, but he found he couldn't. He wasn't going to look his mom in the eye and lie.

"Maybe."

His mom chuckled. "Honey, there's no maybe about it. And for the record, I never saw that look on your face when you were with Amy or Bridget. You might have loved them in a way, but this is different."

"You're right."

"I usually am."

This time he laughed. "I suppose an 'I told you' is coming next."

"Nah, you already said it for me. But I am curious what you're going to do about it."

"I honestly don't know."

"Well, I guess you best get to figuring it out." She glanced over her shoulder. "Saved by another customer."

She started to turn away.

"Mom?"

"Yeah?"

"Thank you."

She looked a tad confused. "For what?"

"Being the best mom a guy could ask for. I always took it for granted, but I realize now that not everyone had that growing up."

She nodded. He had no doubt she knew he was talking about Devon in particular.

"Thank you for being a good son. Now make your mama happy by not letting that girl go."

As he continued to greet visitors and conduct business throughout the rest of the weekend, his mom's words were never far from the front of his mind. He wasn't sure how things would progress between him and Devon in the days to come, but he'd come to the firm conclusion that he had no intention of letting Devon go. Ever.

Chapter Fourteen

Devon danced around her kitchen as she cooked. The past few days had been wonderful. Beyond wonderful. Every moment she spent with Cole was better than the last, and they'd both had a rousing success with the opening weekend of the Arts and Crafts Trail. She'd never seen her store so full of people, and Cole not only sold several of his pieces but he'd also garnered three commissions for large sculptures. One was even going to be displayed in a new art gallery opening in Austin.

All that awesomeness deserved some celebrating, thus her current flurry of cooking and baking. She was going to feed him, then take him to bed. And quite possibly keep him there for a few days. She giggled at the image as she performed some dance moves between the stove and sink.

She noticed Honeysuckle watching her as if she'd lost her mind. "You're just jealous because you don't have a hot date tonight."

Honeysuckle just sneezed and left the room.

Devon was sliding the chocolate cake out of the oven when someone knocked on the door. She squeaked as she looked at the clock. Still too early for Cole, unless he'd decided not to wait until the time she'd given him. No, no, no. That would ruin everything. She wanted everything just right for their special night. A quick glance down at herself, clothed in loose workout pants and a ratty T-shirt, didn't really say *seduction*.

Maybe it was the universe's way of telling her she was getting way too wrapped up in Cole, allowing herself to think of happily-ever-after when he just wanted one day at a time. She took a moment to inhale a deep breath and reminded herself that despite the evening she had planned, she had to keep up the mental wall separating what she and Cole had from thoughts of forever. No matter how nice he was, how much fun they had together, no matter even how much he might like her, she knew his heart. It had been trounced upon twice, and she understood his firm commitment to not getting serious again.

She tossed the hand towel onto the countertop and headed for the door. But when she opened it, her smile quickly faded. Instead of the man who'd captured her heart, it was her mother.

"Mom. What are you doing here?" Her mother rarely came to the farm. She either found Devon in town or summoned her to the ranch.

"We need to talk."

She couldn't very well shut the door in her mother's face, and the sooner she let her mother say whatever she'd come here to say, the sooner she'd leave. Devon opened the door wider and motioned for her mom to come inside.

"Come into the kitchen. I've got things cooking."

Devon went straight to the stove and checked the progress of the oven-barbecued chicken. Her mouth watered at the sight of it.

"Are you having friends over?"

"Just Cole."

Devon got the impression her mother tried to hide her sigh at the mention of his name, but she wasn't successful.

"If this is another attempt to get me to go out with some man you've chosen for me, you can save your breath."

"You act as if I'm trying to ruin your life. I have introduced you to some of the most eligible bachelors in the state, and you turn up your nose at them."

"I've done no such thing. But I'm not going to pretend they're the kind of men I like when they're not."

"How can you know when you barely even speak to them?"

Devon braced her hands on the kitchen island and stared at her mother. "Because I know the type. They're suit-wearing, corporate types. Perhaps they're perfectly nice guys, but that's not what I want."

"No, you want to throw your life away on someone who's probably just trying to get his hands on your family's money. Well, I can tell you one thing, he won't get one red cent."

Devon stared at her mom, stunned into momentary silence. And then the anger rose up to the surface like a geyser blowing. "I cannot believe you just said something so hateful. You don't even really know Cole."

"What was it you said? I know the type."

"You mean someone who is hardworking and has no interest in marrying into money."

"So you don't have a ring yet? I'll admit he's working slower than I anticipated."

"There's not going to be any ring, okay?" Devon's voice rose with the growing anger. "Our relationship is totally casual. And you know what, it didn't even start out as that. In the beginning, we faked it just so you'd leave me alone."

Her mother jerked as if she'd been slapped. "What do you mean?"

"I was sick and tired of you trying to foist all these 'suitable' men on me, and evidently it showed. Cole swooped in to save me, and we became friends. We pretended to date."

Color rose in her mother's cheeks. "But now you're really dating? Maybe he saw what he could have if he made things real."

"Oh, my God! You're not listening to me. Cole doesn't have any interest in getting married. He's tried it twice and neither time worked out."

"Why would you be with someone with whom you have no future?"

"Because he makes me happier than I've ever been."

"But it won't last. You will get hurt."

"Probably."

The look on her mother's face changed. If Devon didn't doubt her own eyesight, she'd swear it softened the tiniest bit.

"Do you love him?"

"Yes." She didn't hesitate, tired of holding the truth inside.

"Devon, I know you're a smart girl. Why would you do this to yourself?"

Devon fought the tears that threatened. "I'd rather be happy with him for a while than to never be happy at all."

Movement beyond her mother drew Devon's attention just as the words left her mouth. Shock hit her hard as she saw Cole, realized he'd heard her. As she realized that she'd probably just ended not only their special night but their relationship, she couldn't hold back the tears anymore. Two fat drops leaked out of her eyes and raced down her cheeks to her chin.

Devon tried to read the expression on Cole's face through her tears. Anger. At her or her mother? And though he might not even be conscious of it, she saw his instinct to turn and run. She tried to smile, to wordlessly tell him that it was okay to do just that, but she simply couldn't manage it. Her heart hurt too much.

Her mother realized he was there and turned toward him and pointed at Devon. "You owe my daughter an apology for breaking her heart."

"Mom!" Devon wanted to shake her mother until she knocked loose some sense, some speck of kindness and understanding.

She expected Cole to turn around and leave. Instead, he stepped more fully into the kitchen and leveled a fierce gaze at her mother.

"No, it's you who owe her an apology. A whole boatload of apologies for not seeing what a kind, generous, brilliant and beautiful woman Devon is."

"How dare you—"

"I dare because it's about damn time someone stands up to you on Devon's behalf. She shouldn't have to constantly tell you that she's entitled to live her life the way she wants to without your meddling."

"I think I know more about what's good for my daughter than you do."

"I don't know why you don't like me, and I frankly couldn't give a rat's ass. But I will not let you hurt Devon anymore. She's a grown woman, and you need to accept her as she is or you're going to lose her for good."

"Is that a threat?"

He shook his head. "No. It's what she's been telling you for a long time that you've not been hearing."

Devon couldn't believe what she was witnessing. If she didn't already love Cole, the way he was defending her would have sealed the deal. He was worth more than all the men her mother had tried to pair her with put together. But a part of her also wished he wasn't rushing to her defense. He had no idea how much harder it was going to be for her to get over losing him because of it.

"I'm her mother. It's my job to protect her, watch out for her best interests."

"No, you're watching out for your best interests. You're more concerned with your status than your daughter's happiness."

"Well, evidently you're not too concerned about her happiness, either. Just using her for a fling."

"She's not just a fling," he said, his voice rising in volume and intensity.

When he slowly turned his head toward Devon, her breath caught. She knew it had to be wishful thinking magnified by the current emotions running high, but she would almost swear she saw her feelings for him reflected back at her.

"I love her."

Devon's world spun. She simply could not have heard him correctly. No, he was back to acting, putting on a really believable show for her mother. While she appreciated it, she wanted to tell him to stop. This was too far for her heart to handle. She couldn't hear him proclaim his love when he didn't mean it.

"Just not enough to make an honest, respectable woman out of her."

Honest and respectable? What century was her mother living in?

"You're wrong again," he said, still looking at Devon so intently that her legs were beginning to literally shake. "If she'll have me, I would love to spend the rest of my life with her." He finally broke eye contact, allowing Devon to catch her breath.

Cole stared at her mother. "And you can keep your money. I don't want a dime of it. Your daughter is worth more than any amount of money or what it can buy."

"Words are cheap."

"You can take mine to the bank."

Before her mother could say anything else, Devon butted in. "Get out."

Her mom glanced at her, then back at Cole. "You heard her."

"I'm talking to you," Devon said.

The expression on her mother's face when she looked back at Devon was a tangle of disbelief and anger. "What?"

"Get...out!"

Devon prepared herself for her mother's next volley, but her mom surprised her by making a disgusted sound and stalking away. Devon was mad enough to slam every door in the house, but her mother closed the door normally behind her, conscious of appearances even while furious.

Devon had never really understood the phrase about silence being deafening until that moment. Before she could collapse, she steadied herself against the island. As her brain cranked away to try to understand how her life had gotten to this holy mess of a point, she shut off the oven. No point in adding burned chicken to the pile of awful.

"Are you okay?" Cole asked as he stepped up to the opposite side of the island.

She didn't meet his gaze. Instead she stared at her hands and wished she could transport herself anywhere but here. A nice deserted island in the South Pacific sounded good right about now. Or the ability to travel back in time so she could tell herself not to get involved with Cole.

"I've been better."

Cole rounded the island and turned her to face him. Only she couldn't force herself to meet his gaze. And she didn't have the strength to resist when he pulled her into his arms. Instead, she wrapped her arms around him and flattened her hands against the muscles in his back. When he dropped a kiss atop her head, she closed her eyes to prevent fresh tears from falling. She couldn't let him know how much she wished the words he'd spoken about loving her were true. As she stood there, knowing their time together was limited, she'd swear she could feel brittle pieces of her heart already shattering.

The longer they stood there, Cole offering her comfort, the more her anger grew. She'd wanted this night to be perfect. Determined to salvage it, especially since it was likely her last opportunity to be with Cole, she pulled away enough to meet his gaze for a moment before kissing him. She poured every last drop of her love for him into the kiss.

In less than the span of a heartbeat, it was as if a fire had been lit between them. Cole framed her face with his strong hands and took the kiss even deeper. She moaned into his mouth, and she'd swear to a room full of judges that she felt an animal-like growl rise up within him, something primal that ignited a thousand flames of desire within her.

She'd planned to end the evening in bed with him. Well, she was moving up the timetable. While continuing to kiss him, she fumbled with the buttons on his shirt. He didn't question her, instead running his hands up her back and unclasping her bra. He lifted his mouth from hers only long enough to remove her shirt and bra, tossing them across the room to land out of sight. At the moment she didn't care if she ever saw them again. When Cole's mouth captured her breast, she decided being naked with this man was the only way to live life.

Needing to feel all of Cole, she backed her way to her bedroom, snatching quick breaths between their kisses.

His mind must have been traveling the same track as hers because moments after they arrived in her room, they were both naked and collapsing into bed. And moments after that, Cole was sliding into her and taking her with a frenzied pace she found she really liked. She responded in kind, digging her fingers into his shoulders as they raced headlong toward world-spinning release.

On the heels of her own peak, she watched as Cole strained above her, the muscles in his neck, chest and arms so taut she didn't think she'd ever seen anything so sexy. As he made one final thrust, she held on to him as if he might disappear if she didn't.

Cole collapsed beside her, his head coming to rest in the crook of her neck. "If I were to die right now, I'd die a happy man."

Why did he have to say things like that when she was trying to prepare herself for losing him? But he did, and she foolishly hung on to those words as if they might mean what she really wanted them to. She needed to bring up what he'd told her mother, but she just couldn't. It was selfish, but she wasn't ready to take that step. Not yet.

"Well, you can't die until you help me eat some of the food I made."

As if on cue, his stomach grumbled.

Devon laughed, surprised she was able to so soon after the ugly scene with her mother. To avoid having Cole possibly bring it up again, she slipped from the bed and grabbed her short cotton robe from the chair in the corner.

"You know, there's no law against eating naked," Cole said from where he stretched out on the bed, putting his strong arms and sculpted chest on drool-inducing display.

Not trusting herself to say anything remotely coherent, she just huffed a quick laugh and walked from the room. She busied herself assembling the food she'd had time to make before her mother and then Cole had shown up. The chicken was still warm in the oven, and she pulled out the potato salad from the fridge.

She looked up at the sound of Cole's footsteps, half expecting him to walk into the kitchen stark naked. Not that she'd mind. He'd pulled on his jeans but left his feet and chest bare, as if he thought that even the jeans wouldn't be on for long.

Devon's cheeks heated in a flash, so she turned to retrieve a couple of glasses from the cabinet. "I had planned to make several more things, but I was interrupted. I did manage to get the cake baked, though."

She braced herself to dive into the inevitable conversation about her mother, her own admission and what Cole had said to her mom. Instead, he stared at the food she'd laid out.

"Were you planning for a dozen people? Because I think we have plenty here."

She tossed a cold roll at him, which he caught, then gave her a wicked grin before taking a bite.

"Those would be better warmed up with some butter," she said.

"They're fine like this. I somehow worked up an appetite."

She loved it when he was flirty and teasing. She'd miss that, along with so many other things about him.

"I can't imagine how."

He moved so quickly around the end of the island toward her that she didn't have time to do anything but squeal, take a couple of awkward steps back and drop two rolls in the floor.

"Look what you made me do."

He pulled her into his arms and grinned wide. "It was worth it."

Cole captured her mouth in another of those kisses that turned her brain to pudding and caused her body temperature to go full-on rocket ignition. She gripped his biceps, partly to steady herself but mainly because she couldn't not touch him. It was as if she'd been searching for a missing piece of herself her entire life and hadn't realized it until Cole had become a part of her world. Her heart screamed for her to ask him to reconsider his view on long-term relationships, to convince him that she was different and worth the risk.

All thought other than the intoxicating feel of his body pressed close to hers fled her brain. She ran her hands over his arms and shoulders, letting her fingers find their way up through his hair. There was no way she'd ever get enough of him.

Time passed as they explored each other, but she couldn't say how much. Eventually, however, hunger of the traditional variety asserted itself. They filled their plates and took them out to her front porch to eat while inhaling the fragrance of the surrounding countryside.

"This is nice," Cole said as he stared out through the deepening night. "I understand why you like it here."

"For a long time, I couldn't explain why exactly this place spoke to me, why it felt so right. But when I came back after visiting my parents one time, it hit me like a lightning bolt. It's the polar opposite of my parents' ranch."

"There's no pretense. What you see is what you get. It's honest, like you."

His words touched something deep inside her heart, but then she felt like a liar. She wasn't telling him the truth, not about how she really felt, how she didn't want to let him go. She was even avoiding bringing up his declaration of love because she feared it had been as false as their initial dates.

Devon didn't know if Cole could tell she was struggling with something or if the timing was coincidence, but he entwined his hand with hers. He didn't say anything, and neither did she. And despite how unsure she was about just about everything but how she felt about him, it was nice to sit quietly with him and let the rhythm and beauty of the night envelop them. When he was gone, she would remember every moment they'd spent together. But it would be this one in particular that she would hold dearest because she didn't think she'd ever felt closer to anyone than she did to Cole right now. She was pretty sure she never would again.

Chapter Fifteen

Devon leaned on her elbow, propping her head on her upturned hand, and watched Cole sleep. She resisted the powerful urge to run her fingers across his stubble-covered cheek because she didn't want to wake him. But the self-control it took to not touch him, to once again curl into his arms and lose herself in his kisses, his hands roaming her body, was substantial. Instead, she watched his slow, even breaths in and out. She smiled at how he'd certainly fallen into a deep sleep after their second round of lovemaking.

Her smile faded, however, when she realized she couldn't avoid getting out of bed any longer. Though it made her a coward, she had to leave before he woke. She'd gone over it again and again in the wee hours and came to the conclusion that she simply wasn't strong enough to say goodbye to him face-to-face. Better to sever the tie without all the awkwardness that would surely make its presence known on their final morning-after. Maybe it would be easier for him, as well. He wouldn't have to explain why he'd professed his love the day before. He'd gone above and beyond to help her, something she could never repay. But she could start by giving him the easy way out.

She slipped from the bed and dressed, not even taking the time to hit the shower. She could use the extra key to Mandy's place after Mandy went to work and shower there, anything to get her away from Cole before he woke up and she was in danger of losing her resolve to do the right thing.

However, she did take the time to write him a note. There was no way to say everything that was in her heart, but she wouldn't leave him without even a word of profound thanks.

Tears filled her eyes as she folded the note, wrote his name on the outside, took a precious moment to run her fingertips over his name, and then propped the note against a flower vase on the kitchen island.

"Goodbye, Cole," she whispered, then made her way quietly out the front door.

EVEN BEFORE HE opened his eyes, he could smell her, the unique scent of vanilla and woman that belonged to Devon alone. Beneath the sheet covering his lower half, certain parts of his anatomy sprang to life. He'd not been a monk by any stretch since he'd first lost his virginity back during high school, but he couldn't recall ever having such an insatiable desire for a woman. Not even either of his wives. But Devon was different, someone he wouldn't have ever paired himself with if anyone had asked but who had managed to effortlessly fill all the empty spaces in his life. In his heart.

And she'd told her mother that she loved him. Only days ago that revelation would have sent him fleeing. Truth was it still scared him more than a little, same as his own feelings for her. But the thought of letting her go was way worse.

Somewhere in the midst of their time together, he'd started falling for Devon. He could tell himself it was a bad idea all he wanted, but it wasn't going to change the truth. Then there was the voice in his head telling him that this time it was different, that the third time really was the charm. It made sense in a way because Devon was nothing like Amy or Bridget. She was giving where they were selfish, kind while they were snappish, happy with a simple, rewarding life while his exes never had enough.

How had he been such a fool not only once but twice? That didn't say great things about his intelligence. But when he looked at Devon, touched her, inhaled her scent, listened to her laugh, texted with her late at night, he felt as if he'd be a bigger fool if he let her go.

His mom was right. It hadn't worked out with Amy or Bridget because they weren't right for him. Everything had been leading him to Devon. But what if it didn't work out? Even the thought of it twisted him into painful knots inside.

His thoughts went back to how his admission of his feelings had simply popped out during the argument with her mother. It was a terrible time and place to confess such a thing. Devon deserved something romantic instead. But the admission had burst forth from him without him even thinking about it, as if it could no longer be contained. And he'd been surprised afterward when he hadn't wanted to call back the words. Even more surprised at how relieved and lighter he felt for having said them.

How would Devon react if he told her again, this time without her bitch of a mother watching and judging?

Perhaps it was time he found out.

He rolled over to discover that Devon wasn't on the other side of the bed. When he lifted himself halfway and listened, he didn't hear the shower or movement in the other parts of the house. Maybe she was outside checking on her animals. It hit him that normally he'd be out doing the same thing by now and that his mom was going to know exactly what happened since he didn't come home the night before.

Cole ran a hand over his face, then slipped from the bed and pulled on his jeans. He headed for the front door but glanced toward the kitchen. A piece of paper with his name on it was sitting next to a flower vase. He smiled as he imagined her leaving some sort of sweet note for him to find, maybe inviting him outside for some more heat-filled kissing.

But when he opened the paper, it took only a moment to realize the note was something entirely different.

> *Cole,*
> *I'm sorry for leaving without saying goodbye,*
> *but I believe this will be easier for both of us.*
> *Thank you so much for all your help, for being*
> *such a good friend. You'll never know how much*
> *it's meant to me, how you did more than I could*
> *have ever expected. You're a good man, and I*
> *wish you nothing but the best.*
> *Devon*

He dropped the paper, his insides suddenly hollow. He'd been a fool. Again.

THREE DAYS LATER, Cole stepped out of the bank to find Mandy waiting for him.

"Do you know where Devon is?"

After a momentary pause, he moved to step past her. "No."

Mandy grabbed his arm with surprising strength. "What happened? Did you end things with her?"

He didn't make eye contact, instead looking straight ahead. "You've got that backward."

Her grip lessened but she didn't let go. "I don't understand."

This time he did look down at her. "We both knew it would end. She ended it." He heard way more hurt and anger in his voice than he cared to admit.

"Yeah, I'm going to need a bit more than that because I haven't seen or heard from her in three days."

Despite his anger, which was truthfully aimed more at himself for being three times the fool, a wave of concern hit him. "What do you mean? She's not been to work?"

"No. She texted me that she was taking some time off, but she's not responding to phone calls or texts."

"She's probably doing her hermit thing at home."

Mandy was already shaking her head. "She's not there. She asked me to take care of her animals until she got back."

That concern in his middle ratcheted up a notch. He might be upset about how things had ended, but he'd yet to find the off switch for how he felt about Devon.

"Maybe she's at her parents' place."

"You and I both know that's the last place she'd go if she's upset."

He glanced around downtown, as if Devon might suddenly appear. Could she have been telling the truth when she'd told her mother she loved him? Over the past few days, he'd convinced himself it was just a really good act on her part. But what if it wasn't?

"What happened?" Mandy asked.

Unwilling to air the details in the middle of the flow

of people entering and exiting the bank, he walked toward where he'd parked. Mandy followed, probably wondering if he was going to leave without answering her question. When he reached his truck, he gripped the side of the bed and gave her the truncated version of events.

"Have you tried to reach her?" she asked.

"Yes. I called, texted. No answer. I figured that was my answer, that she doesn't feel the way I do."

"But she told her mother that she loved you."

The tone of Mandy's voice told him exactly how big of an idiot she thought he was, and in that moment, he was inclined to agree with her.

"I thought it was all part of the act for her mom."

"You big dope, Devon has been in love with you almost from the beginning."

"She never said that."

"Of course not. You'd made it abundantly clear you were never going to get married again. And despite the poor example she had growing up, Devon wants a husband and children. She wants the type of loving family she never had."

He gripped the metal of the truck so hard that he wouldn't be surprised if it buckled. "Where could she be?"

"I have no idea."

If she was hurt somewhere, alone, he'd never forgive himself.

DEVON TOOK ONE more lingering look at Blue Falls Lake from the overlook before turning back toward her car. She'd been gone for a week, giving herself time to think, away from everything and everyone familiar. It had taken hours of sitting on the beach at North Padre, just listening to the waves and not having to speak to anyone or be responsible for anything for her to get her head back on straight. She'd considered making a move away from Blue Falls, but after several days of crying and wandering aimlessly, the truth had settled within her. Blue Falls was home, always would be. She'd just have to learn to cope with seeing Cole on occasion.

But hopefully not too soon. Despite the time away, her heart was still raw from that particular loss. And she had no one to blame but herself. Not even her mother. Devon had been the one to initiate the relationship, and now she had to live with the consequences.

When she slipped into the driver's seat, she turned on her phone for the first time since she'd texted Mandy that she was taking some time off. Not surprisingly there were dozens of messages, mostly from Mandy. Her heart jolted when she saw a few from Cole. Not feeling up to reading or listening to any of them now, she tossed the phone back into her purse and headed toward home.

Even though she hadn't worked in a week, an overwhelming fatigue hit her as she approached her house. But a jolt of adrenaline hit her when she spotted Cole's truck parked in her driveway. What was he doing here? She considered turning around and leaving again, but she'd already taken the coward's way out with him once. She wouldn't do it again.

But she didn't have a chance to prepare what she was going to say to him because as soon as she stepped out of the car, he strode toward her from the barn. He dropped a bucket of milk, letting it spill down the hillside behind him. His long legs ate up the space between them faster than she could form coherent thoughts.

"Cole—" It was all she got out before he pulled her into his arms and held her close.

"Thank God you're all right."

For a moment, she couldn't pull away. It felt too good to have his arms around her, something she hadn't expected to ever feel again. But the longer she let him hug her, the harder it would be to step back. So she extricated herself.

"Why are you here?" she asked.

"Taking care of your animals."

"I asked Mandy to do that."

"She has been, but I told her I'd help since she's also been running the store alone."

A shard of guilt stabbed Devon. She had a lot of apologizing to do to her best friend.

"She's been worried sick about you," Cole said. "So have I. Where have you been?"

"I needed some time off."

"Suddenly, the morning after I said I loved you?"

She shook her head. "I don't understand why you're upset. I know you were helping me out with Mom. I—"

He closed the gap between them again and gripped her shoulders, not hard but firm. "What I said was the truth, every bit of it. And I'll say it again. I love you."

"But you said you didn't want…" She shook her head, unwilling to hope that he was telling the truth.

Cole slipped one of his hands up to cup her cheek. "I changed my mind." His other hand came up to the opposite side of her face. "You changed my mind." He ran a thumb across her cheek.

Her mind spun until she felt dizzy. Was this really happening? "I can't handle it if you change your mind again."

He smiled. "I won't. I couldn't even stop loving you

when you disappeared and I thought it had all been an act to you. But I need to know for sure, do you feel the same? Did you mean what you told your mom?"

She stared up at him, her insides quaking. "Yes." It came out as a whisper, but it evidently was enough because Cole pulled her close and kissed her like he couldn't get enough of her.

Devon had just started to kiss him back when he scooped her up into his arms and carried her toward the house. She yelped in surprise.

"What are you doing?"

"Showing you just how much I love you."

And this time, she wasn't going to run away.

DEVON'S SENSES SLOWLY woke one by one, as if they were being gradually turned on via switches. First hearing as she heard a bird chirping away outside and the white noise that came from living in an electrified world. Touch. Her body felt used, but in a good way. Memories of making love with Cole, the way he'd made her feel as if he worshipped everything about her, including her body, came into focus in her mind, making her smile. Yes, a very good way. She rolled over, expecting to find the warmth of one incredibly sexy man next to her. But all she encountered was emptiness.

Sight. Her eyelids lifted to reveal the truth, causing an ache to bloom in her chest. The opposite side of the bed was rumpled and she could smell his distinctive male scent lingering in the air, but Cole was gone. She pushed away the instinctive panic. There was no way he had faked what they'd shared. She hated the tiny ember of doubt that refused to be extinguished.

After dressing in a loose pair of cotton lounge pants and a T-shirt, then brushing her teeth, she made her way out to the kitchen. Still no Cole. Was this how he'd felt when he'd awakened to find she'd left him? Guilt stung her like a swarm of bees.

Some sound she wasn't used to hearing drew her attention outside. As she walked toward the front door, she realized it was a voice. She stepped out onto the front porch and immediately spotted Cole in the pasture with the goats and sheep. She couldn't help but chuckle at the apparent one-sided conversation he was having with them.

A peaceful feeling of warmth and rightness drifted through her. Though Cole looked at home on his ranch, he appeared comfortable here, as well. For a few moments, she allowed herself to imagine waking up every morning knowing that Cole was either lying next to her or nearby.

As she made her way toward him, she let her gaze wander over his tall, powerful frame. He might not be able to ride bulls anymore, but Cole was still strong, still every inch a desirable man. Her skin heated at the memory of his body moving over and within her the night before. She'd imagined making love to him before they'd taken their relationship to that level, but all those daydreams didn't even approach reality.

He must have heard her because he turned to look in her direction and smiled. "Look who finally woke up."

She lifted a brow, causing him to smile even wider.

"I didn't expect to find you talking to the animals when I got up," she said.

He scratched between the ears of Gertrude, one of the goats. "They're very good listeners."

"That right? Now I've got to hear what fascinating topic you and the critters were conversing about."

Cole walked toward her, stopping on the opposite

side of the fence, close enough to lean forward to kiss her if he wanted.

"You," he said.

"Oh yeah? Do they have demands and you're their representative?"

He chuckled. "No, I was asking for some advice."

"From goats and sheep?"

He shrugged. "They were handy. And they let me talk without interrupting."

A slight inflection in his voice, in the way he was looking at her, told her something was going on behind his teasing.

She took a couple of steps back as Cole climbed over the fence. Her breath grew shaky as he erased the distance between them.

His lips tipped up slightly at the edges as he reached to cup her jaw and run his thumb across her bottom lip. "What I told your mother was one hundred percent true, all of it. I won't lie and say I came here planning to tell you that I love you and that I want to spend the rest of my life with you, but when I said the words they felt righter than anything I've ever said."

Cole lowered his mouth to hers. The kiss felt like a pledge that the things he'd said were true, from his heart.

"Are you sure?" she asked against his lips.

He stepped back from her but didn't break the contact between them. With her hands clasped in his, he slowly eased himself to one knee in front of her. A whimper of surprise escaped her, and he squeezed her hands gently in response.

"I didn't think I'd ever want to marry again, but my mom was right. She said it didn't work out before because I hadn't found the right woman. Now I have."

"How do you know that? Maybe all the pretending has you confused."

He was already shaking his head before she finished speaking.

"I've never been more positive about anything." He pulled something from his jeans pocket, something small and circular. "I will get you a real one if you'd rather have it, but I made this while you were gone. I kept hoping I'd have a chance to give it to you." He held up a ring made of two pieces of wire intertwined like vines with tiny metal flowers attached. How had his big hands made something so delicate?

"Will you marry me, Devon Newberry?"

She stared down at him, her heart beating fast and hard. "Tell me I'm not dreaming this."

Cole smiled up at her. "Would it be a good or bad dream?"

"Good. Very good." She slipped one of her hands free of his and let her fingers drift along the edge of his face, trying to convince herself that he was real and this wasn't a dream. "Yes."

"Yes, what?"

She smiled, her heart filling with a feeling of such intense joy she didn't think there was a way it could hold it all. "Yes, I'll marry you, Cole Davis. And I don't want another ring. This one is perfect."

Though it defied biology, her heartbeat increased even more as Cole slipped the ring he'd fashioned onto her finger. She took it as a good sign that it fit perfectly. Then he stood slowly and framed her face with both of his hands.

"I love you, Devon. Don't ever doubt it."

"I love you, too, so much."

She squealed when he lifted her in his arms and swung her around. "Don't hurt your back!"

He didn't return her to the ground. "Sweetheart, if you were going to hurt my back, it was going to happen last night."

A fierce blush rushed up her neck into her entire face.

Cole chuckled then kissed her like a man in love.

Devon was on the verge of dragging him back to bed when the sound of a vehicle slowing down on the road pulled her out of her lust-filled haze.

When she recognized her parents' expensive black SUV, she dropped her head against Cole's chest and groaned. Why did her mother have to show up and ruin this moment, the single best day of Devon's life?

Cole rubbed up and down her back. "I'll take care of it."

She lifted her forehead from his chest. "No, I'll do it. She's my mother."

But when Devon turned to face the vehicle, it wasn't her mother who stepped out but her father. Graham Newberry was six-foot-four of "get things done." Devon always equated her father with work, whether that meant he was schmoozing while wearing an expensive suit, overseeing work at the Diamond Ranch Western Wear facilities, or in the saddle surveying his tens of thousands of acres of ranchland. He wasn't a harsh man, but he wasn't the warm and fuzzy type, either. Because he was always busy was the reason Devon had spent so much more time with her mother while growing up.

Her dad was already sizing up Cole before he stepped out of the SUV, before his five-hundred-dollar boots hit the driveway. Had her mother really felt the need to send her dad out here as a second wave of attack? How had her mom even known she was home? Devon thought back to the time when Cole had asked her why she'd stuck around Blue Falls. Now she was asking herself the same question again.

"Hello, Dad," she said as her father approached. She admittedly didn't put a lot of warmth and welcome into the greeting.

"Devon." He shifted his steely gaze to Cole. "Mr. Davis."

"Mr. Newberry." Cole placed his arm around Devon's shoulders and tugged her gently to his side.

"Before you think your mother sent me here to do her bidding," her dad said, ever astute, "I want you to know that she won't be butting her nose into your business anymore."

Devon couldn't have heard him correctly. "Has hell frozen over and I didn't hear about it?"

Well, she hadn't intended that to pop out, but something about having Cole's reassuring presence next to her gave her an added boost of courage.

"Not the last I heard, but I did let her know in no uncertain terms that it was time she let you live your life as you see fit."

"And she agreed?"

"Let's say she's not happy about it, but then she also thought she would get my support when she asked me to come 'talk some sense into you.'"

Devon's world felt as if it had been tossed inside the spin cycle of a washing machine that happened to be tumbling down the side of a mountain at the same time. She couldn't recall her father ever stepping in on her behalf with her mother.

He took a couple of steps toward her, and she felt compelled to meet his gaze.

"I'm sorry that I've never done this for you before. And I don't have an excuse. I guess I always told myself that you were strong enough to stand up for yourself and you didn't need your daddy to do it for you."

"She is strong," Cole said before Devon could speak. "The strongest woman I've ever met. And the kindest."

"But that doesn't mean she didn't need the support of her father." Her dad nodded once at the understanding that seemed to be passing between him and Cole. "Is it true? Do you love my daughter?"

"I do, very much." No hesitation, none at all.

"Good. Devon deserves to have someone to love her unconditionally, someone who won't be so consumed with other things that her needs are overlooked."

"That won't happen. And just so you know, I've asked her to be my wife and she's accepted."

Her father stared at Cole for such an endless moment that Devon's insides knotted until they cramped. Cole's revelation filled her to bursting with love for him, but she wondered how her father would take it. Would he expect Cole to ask his permission?

Instead, her dad shifted his focus to her. "Are you happy?"

"Yes."

He nodded again. "That's good enough for me." He extended his hand to Cole, who accepted it in a firm shake. "Your father was a good man, so I have no doubt that you are, as well. I'm sorry if my wife made you feel otherwise."

When he released Cole's hand, her dad came closer to her and gripped her shoulders. "I want to apologize for how your mother and I have failed you."

Out of some instinct to make others feel better, she started to speak, but her father beat her to it.

"We both got too caught up in other things and neglected what was really important, getting to know our child and making sure she was not only cared for but also happy. That ends today." He glanced at Cole, then back to her. "And I promise you that if you have children, they will know their grandparents love them. But they will be yours to raise as you see fit."

"I doubt Mom will be happy about that."

"She will either accept things as they are or continue to be miserable. It's her choice."

Her mother was miserable? But as her father's words sank into Devon's brain like water through a sponge, they made a depressing kind of sense. When was the last time she'd seen her mother actually happy? Oh, she was good at pasting on a smile and playing the role of executive wife, but Devon realized she hadn't a clue what would make her mother happy. Not just satisfied with appearances but truly happy. Devon had been so focused on how her mother treated her that she'd been totally unaware that there might be a deeper reason for why her mother acted the way she did.

Her dad surprised her by leaning forward and planting a kiss on Devon's forehead. "I'm happy for you."

As he walked back to the SUV and drove away, Devon watched and marveled that at least one of her parents was happy about her relationship with Cole. But she was left with a nagging feeling that in order to truly move forward and find that forever kind of happiness that she'd long dreamed about, she had to find a way for her mother to claim her own.

Chapter Sixteen

"Are you sure you don't want me to go with you?" Cole asked.

Devon stood on the driver's side of her car with the door open and looked up into the face she loved more every day.

"No, this is something I need to do on my own." She'd taken a week after her father's appearance at her house to think through several scenarios, knowing she'd likely have only one chance to get this right.

"Call if you need me."

"Thank you." She pushed up onto her toes and kissed him where he stood on the other side of the door.

But as she drove to the small winery at the edge of the county, her stomach churned with anxiety. She hadn't had a lot of success throughout the years of having conversations with her mother that didn't end with some level of disagreement. To minimize the chances of any conversation blowing up, she'd arranged to meet her mom on neutral but public ground. The cozy eatery housed at the Wild Blooms Winery would afford them a semblance of privacy to talk but without it being so private the conversation was doomed to fail. And Devon was determined that it wouldn't, if at all possible. Everything in her life was truly wonderful now, all except the strained relationship with her mother.

She didn't want her life with Cole to be periodically torpedoed by something her mother did or said. And the more she thought about it, the more she believed her mother must be truly unhappy to behave the way she did. The problem would be getting her mother to admit it, convincing her to open up and change. Though Devon felt deeply that this was the right thing to do, for both of them, she didn't look forward to the process.

She wanted to luxuriate in the fact that Cole really loved her, that he was willing to take a third chance at marriage because of that love. Each morning since he'd proposed, she'd awakened afraid it had all been a dream. But when she either saw Cole next to her or received a flirty text from him, she'd relax and marvel that she'd gotten so lucky.

Devon made her way up the entrance road, momentarily struck by how lovely the stone winery and the vineyards stretching out in the distance were. The atmosphere was posh enough to satisfy her mother but peaceful and beautiful as Devon preferred.

She was glad to see it wasn't very busy when she pulled into the parking area. Her mother's car was parked in the first slot, and as Devon walked toward the building, she saw her mom sitting on the patio with a glass of wine.

"You're late."

Devon resisted the urge to meet the barb with one of her own. She knew good and well she was on time, that her mother had arrived early, but she let it go. Instead, she slipped into the seat opposite her mother and ordered her own glass of wine along with some bruschetta.

"Your father tells me you're engaged, so no need to tell me if that's why you've called me here."

Her mother certainly wasn't going to make this easy, but Devon marshaled her determination to see her plan through.

"I am. He's a good man, Mom. I love him and he loves me."

"I thought it was all pretending just to spite me."

"Initially, but not to spite you. I just wanted a little peace from our disagreements. But the pretending gave way to real affection, then love. I'm happy, and I want you to be happy for me."

Her mother gave her a look of surprise, her forehead crinkling and her head tilting slightly to the side.

On instinct, Devon reached across the table and placed her hand atop her mother's well-manicured one. "I know we have rarely seen eye to eye, but I do love you, Mom. I want us to have a better relationship, and… I want you to be happy, too."

"I find that hard to believe since you balk at every suggestion I make."

Devon shook her head slowly. "I don't think having me follow in your footsteps will make you happy."

"And I suppose you think you know what will."

"No, but I'd like for you to find it. I've been doing a lot of thinking, and the more I think about it the more I believe something in the past made you really unhappy and you haven't let go of it."

Her mother looked at her as if she thought Devon had been body snatched. Before she could say anything, however, Devon continued.

"I can't remember ever seeing you really happy. Maybe something bordering on content, but not true happiness, not like what I feel when I'm with Cole."

Devon hesitated for a moment, bracing herself for what was sure to be an explosive response from her mother. "Are you and Dad not happy together?"

The response Devon had expected didn't come. Instead, her mother slowly turned her head to stare off toward the vineyard and the ribbon of river snaking through the countryside beyond it. Devon didn't press her mom to respond, instead remaining quiet and still.

"No one's ever asked me that, not even your father," her mom said in a voice so small that Devon doubted she'd recognize it if she weren't staring right at her mother. She sounded far away, as if she were watching a movie of the past in her mind.

"Tell me what happened."

Her mom seemed to snap back to the present and pulled her hands into her lap. "It's nothing. I have everything I could ever want."

Devon wasn't letting her mom off the hook that easily. "Things, yes, but that's not what makes life worth living."

"So you'd be happy without your little farm and your yarn shop?"

"I do love those things and they make me happy, but if they went away and I still had Cole I'd still be overjoyed."

"He may not feel the same way."

"He does." She said it with the conviction she felt. Devon no longer doubted Cole's feelings for her or his commitment.

"How do you know? Men can make you believe what isn't true."

It was Devon's turn to tilt her head in search of the meaning behind the words. "Did something happen between you and Dad?"

Her mother remained silent as the waitress brought Devon's wine and bruschetta to the table. But as soon as the young woman was out of earshot, Devon returned her attention to her mom.

"Why are you pressing this?" her mother asked.

"Because I'm going to be married, Mom, and I hope to eventually have kids. I want them to have a good relationship with their grandparents, and that means you and I have to get beyond whatever has always stood between us. I won't subject my kids to what I've gone through."

"What you've gone through? You sound as if we abused you."

"You did." Devon hadn't realized until the words left her mouth that that's how she'd viewed the way her mother treated her. If she was asking her mother for the truth, she had to give it in return. So everything poured out, how Devon had never felt as if she measured up, how her mother didn't attempt to understand her and her choices, even how the ache inside her had led to her being overweight and trying to hide it in high school.

When Devon finally finished speaking, her mom looked stunned. Slowly, she retrieved her purse and placed cash on the table.

Devon's heart hurt that her mother could hear all of what she'd said and then just leave without a response. But instead of heading toward her car, her mother took the stone path that led in the opposite direction, through the vineyards toward a gazebo by the river. Devon watched her mom, completely at a loss at her mother's reaction and whether she should follow her.

She gave herself a couple of minutes, taking a few sips of the wine but not touching the bruschetta. After dropping her own payment on the table, she stood, took a deep breath and followed the same path.

By the time she caught up, her mom was already standing in the gazebo watching the gentle flow of the river. Devon went to stand beside her. Neither of them spoke for so long that Devon wondered if her mother was going to remain silent until Devon got tired of waiting and left.

"I got lost," her mom said suddenly, surprising Devon.

She glanced at her mother, whose gaze was still fixed on the river. "What do you mean?"

Her mom let out a long, slow breath, as if that was the last wall to collapse that had been hiding the truth.

"Before your father, I was in love with someone else." She shook her head. "At least I thought I was. It was…" She hesitated for so long that it seemed she might be reconsidering divulging anything else. "It was Cole's father."

Devon couldn't help the sound of shock that escaped her.

Her mom held up a hand to forestall any questions. "It was well before he married Barbara. We went out, once. I fancied myself in love with him, but he soon fell for Barbara."

"That's why the two of you don't like each other?"

A single nod. "I let it fester, and it's been so long I can't even remember why. But I do remember thinking that I would show them. When I met your father, I made it my mission to win him."

A pit opened up inside Devon. "You didn't love him? He was just another acquisition?"

To her credit, her mother lowered her head and seemed to shrink. Though Devon couldn't see her mother's full expression, she believed it to be one of shame.

"Have you ever loved him?"

"I grew to love him, yes, but…" She brought her palms up to cover her face for a few seconds before lowering them again. "By the time I realized it, I think he'd given up and buried himself in work. And I…I tried to find happiness in other ways without realizing it."

"So he loved you from the beginning?"

Her mom nodded. "Seems I have developed a track record for disappointing those who love me."

Part of Devon wanted to comfort her mother, but she was right. "It's never too late to change."

"I'm not sure that's true. It's been so long since your father and I have even had a real conversation."

Devon turned her mother to face her. "Do you want to make it work with him?"

Her mom stared at her for a few seconds, as if she could find the answer in Devon's eyes. Then she slowly nodded. "But I don't know how."

In that moment, her mother looked like someone who had to make it to the other side of the river but had no clue how to swim.

"Perhaps you just tell him the truth. It does wonders." Devon smiled, realizing she couldn't remember the last time she'd had a smile for her mom.

For her mom's part, she looked as surprised to see it as Devon was to give it. Devon wished this was the part where she and her mom would hug and all would be well, but things didn't magically get better that quickly in real life. But she felt as if they'd taken the biggest, most important step toward arriving at that point.

Epilogue

Devon couldn't stop pacing back and forth across the bedroom that had been hers when she was a child. Halfway through another pass, her mother stepped in front of her, halting her progress.

"You're going to carve a trench in the carpet."

"I can't help it. I feel like the jitters are going to consume me."

Her mother clasped Devon's hands between hers and smiled. She did that a bit more often now, two months after their conversation in the winery gazebo. They still had a ways to go and her mom still gave her unsolicited opinion on occasion, but at least they were moving in the right direction. Devon no longer dreaded seeing her mom's name on caller ID, and her mom was trying to learn about the life choices Devon had made. She was even allowing Devon to teach her how to knit.

"You might not believe me, but I was nervous on my wedding day, too. Granted, it was different, but I think most brides are nervous."

Part of Devon wanted to ask about why her mother's nervousness was different from her own, but she didn't broach the subject. Her mother needed time to gradually open up and share, and Devon allowed her that. One didn't change overnight.

"I just want this done so I can stop feeling like I'm going to vibrate out of my skin."

"Don't wish this away too quickly. Learn from my mistakes and pay attention to each moment. Don't let the good ones pass you by without you noticing."

Her mom took a couple of steps back and spread Devon's arms out so she could look at Devon's dress, a white, asymmetrical cotton one with lace trim that harkened back to the 1800s but with a modern flair. Though her mother had made her wish known for her to wear a more traditional wedding gown and have a big wedding, she'd eventually agreed to a smaller affair if she could host it at Diamond Ranch.

"It's not what I would have chosen, but I'll admit it's lovely," her mom said. "India has an eye for pieces that shouldn't be fashionable but are."

A knock at the door proved to be Barbara. She poked her head in. "It's almost time." She stopped before saying anything else and looked at Devon in awe as she stepped into the room. "Darling, you look gorgeous. We'll be lucky if Cole doesn't scoop you up and race off with you before you finish the vows."

"He better not," Devon's mom said.

Barbara just chuckled. "Don't worry. I raised him better than that."

Though there were still hints of tension between the two women, for the most part they'd agreed to leave the past in the past and get along for their children's sake. They'd actually worked together on planning the wedding with less than two months to do so.

Devon's dad showed up then. "Time to take your seats, ladies."

Barbara offered Devon a smile and a blown kiss before she exited the room. Devon's mom lingered a little longer. When she placed her palm against Devon's cheek, the tenderness of the gesture filled Devon's heart.

"I'm sorry I was not the mother I should have been when you needed me to be. I'm glad you were stronger than me and forced me to see a different path."

Devon blinked against tears. "I love you, Mom."

"I love you, too, dear. Now I better go sit down so that you can make your way to someone else who loves you."

When her mom left the room, Devon took a moment to rein in her emotions before turning toward her dad.

"You look gorgeous," he said. "So much like your mother on our wedding day." The light in his eyes, like he was drifting back to that long-ago day, brought a smile to Devon's face.

"Things are better between you and Mom?"

He gripped her shoulders gently. "Yes, thanks to you. Seems we raised a child smarter and more mature than either of us." He leaned forward and kissed her on the forehead, then offered her his arm. "Shall we?"

As they made their way downstairs and to the conservatory, which was gorgeously decorated with thousands of white lights and four different Christmas trees, her heart tried its best to beat out of her chest. When she saw Cole standing at the front next to Cooper, he took her breath away. He wore the same suit he had the night he'd danced with her in this room, the night they'd first made love. She'd swear she walked on clouds as her father led her closer to Cole.

When her dad left her with Cole in front of the minister, her soon-to-be husband leaned toward her and whispered, "You look beautiful."

"Not too bad yourself, cowboy."

He smiled, and her heart overflowed with love,

filling the rest of her body and soul. That standing-on-clouds feeling continued as they made their way through the vows. It took all her effort, but she heeded her mother's advice and paid attention to every moment, every word, every sensation as Cole held her hands and then as he kissed her after they were declared husband and wife.

"I love you," he said against her lips at the end of the kiss.

"I love you more."

He smiled. "Not possible."

As they turned to face the assembled guests, she noticed the happy looks on her parents' faces and the fact that they were holding hands. In that moment, Devon Newberry Davis knew she couldn't ask for anything more. She already had it all.

* * * * *

Look for more stories in Trish Milburn's
BLUE FALLS, TEXAS *series in 2017!*

Western Romance

Available November 8, 2016

#1617 A TEXAS COWBOY'S CHRISTMAS
Texas Legacies: The Lockharts
by Cathy Gillen Thacker
Single mom Molly Griffith and rancher Chance Lockhart have never gotten along, until Molly's three-year-old son's unrealistic expectations—wanting a baby bull for Christmas—unite them!

#1618 THE CHRISTMAS TRIPLETS
Cupid's Bow, Texas • by Tanya Michaels
Will Trent is temporarily looking after a baby and needs help from his neighbor Megan Rivers, a single mom who seems to hate him. How can he prove to her he's not the playboy she thinks he is?

#1619 THE COWBOY'S CHRISTMAS BRIDE
Hope, Montana • by Patricia Johns
Andy Granger, the prodigal cowboy, has returned to Hope, Montana. The townsfolk aren't ready to forgive his betrayal... least of all Dakota Mason. But Andy's willing to try anything to get into the beautiful rancher's good graces!

#1620 A FAMILY IN WYOMING
The Marshall Brothers • by Lynnette Kent
Susannah Bradley finds refuge from her abusive husband on Wyatt Marshall's ranch—and discovers an unexpected attraction to the gruff rancher. But if she stays, will she just bring terror to Wyatt's doorstep?

REQUEST YOUR FREE BOOKS!

2 FREE NOVELS PLUS 2 FREE GIFTS!

HARLEQUIN®

Western Romance

ROMANCE THE ALL-AMERICAN WAY!

Western Romance

*Single mom Molly Griffith and rancher
Chance Lockhart have never gotten along, until Molly's
three-year-old son's Christmas wish unites them!*

Read on for a sneak preview of
A TEXAS COWBOY'S CHRISTMAS,
book two of Cathy Gillen Thacker's popular miniseries
TEXAS LEGACIES: THE LOCKHARTS.

"So you're really not going to help me?"

"Convince your son he doesn't want to be a cowboy? And have a ranch like mine? Or get a head start on it by getting his first livestock now?" Chance's provoking grin widened. "No. I will, however, try to talk him into getting a baby calf. Since females are a lot more docile than males."

"Ha-ha."

"I wasn't talking about you," he claimed with choirboy innocence.

Yeah...right. When they were together like this, *everything* was about the two of them.

Molly forced her attention back to her child's fervent wish to be a rancher, just like "Cowboy Chance." Who was, admittedly, the most heroic-looking figure her son had ever met.

"I live in town, remember? I don't have any place to keep a baby calf. And even if it were possible, Braden and I aren't going to be here past the first week of January."

Squinting curiously, he matched his strides to hers.

"How come?"

Trying not to notice how he towered over her, or how much she liked it, Molly fished her keys out of her pocket. "Not that it's any of your business, but we're moving to Dallas."

Chance paused next to her vehicle. "To be closer to Braden's daddy?"

Her heart panged in her chest. If only her little boy had a father who wanted his child in his life. But he didn't, so...

There was no way she was talking to Chance Lockhart about the most humiliating mistake she'd ever made. Or the fact that her ill-conceived liaison had unexpectedly led to the best thing in her life. "No."

"No, that's not why you're moving?"

He came close enough she could smell the soap and sun and man fragrance of his skin.

Awareness shimmered inside her.

He watched her open the car door. "Or no, that's not what you want—to be closer to your ex?"

Heavens, the man was annoying!

Figuring this was the time to go on record with her goals—and hence vanquish his mistaken notions about her once and for all—Molly looked up. "What I want is for my son to grow up with all the advantages I never had." Braden, unlike her, would want for nothing.

Except maybe a daddy in his life.

Don't miss
A TEXAS COWBOY'S CHRISTMAS
by Cathy Gillen Thacker, available November 2016
everywhere Harlequin® Western Romance®
books and ebooks are sold.

www.Harlequin.com

Wrangle Your Friends for the
Ultimate Ranch Girls' Getaway

Win an all-expenses-paid 3-night luxurious stay for you and your 3 guests at The Resort at Paws Up in Greenough, Montana.

Retail Value $10,000

A TOAST TO FRIENDSHIP, AN ADVENTURE OF A LIFETIME!

Learn more at www.Harlequinranchgetaway.com

Sweepstakes ends August 31, 2016

WCHMR

HARLEQUIN®

A *Romance* FOR EVERY MOOD™

JUST CAN'T GET ENOUGH?

Join our social communities
and talk to us online.

You will have access to the latest
news on upcoming titles and special
promotions, but most importantly,
you can talk to other fans about your
favorite Harlequin reads.

Harlequin.com/Community

Facebook.com/HarlequinBooks

Twitter.com/HarlequinBooks

Pinterest.com/HarlequinBooks

Love the Harlequin book you just read?

Your opinion matters.

Review this book on your favorite book site, review site, blog or your own social media properties and share your opinion with other readers!